**Books written by Sally M. Russell:**

An Escape for Joanna
\* Finding a Path to Happiness
\* Dr. Wilder's Only True Love
\* Josh and the Mysterious Princess
\* A Summer's Adventure
A Surprise Awaits Back Home
The Attorney and his Untamed Tigress

\* Haven of Rest Ranch Series

# The
# Attorney
## and the
# Untamed
# Tigress

SALLY M. RUSSELL

authorHOUSE®

AuthorHouse™ LLC
1663 Liberty Drive
Bloomington, IN 47403
www.authorhouse.com
Phone: 1-800-839-8640

Published by AuthorHouse 10/18/2013

ISBN: 978-1-4918-2813-7 (sc)
ISBN: 978-1-4918-2812-0 (e)

Library of Congress Control Number: 2013918560

**This book is dedicated to:**

First, to my husband, J.T., who was determined to take a boat trip down to the Gulf of Mexico. It had been his dream for years. Second, to all the boat owners at Hamm's Holiday Harbor, Chillicothe, IL, who listened to his plans and never uttered a discouraging word although a few of them had started on similar trips only to return when problems occurred. They were actually doubtful that J.T., at 72, was going to be successful, but how thrilled they were when we returned the following year with a completed round-trip river cruise to tell them about.

"Oh, Honey,

that coffee sure smells good," Cory said as he approached her with that cute smile he was hoping would dazzle her now like it usually had.

"Don't honey me, Cory Calhoun. Until I know what has been going on around here, these 2 cups of coffee remain with me unless I decide to douse the two of you with them."

There is a time for everything, and a season for every activity under heaven: there is a time to be silent and a time to speak.

Ecclesiastes 3:1, 7b

## Chapter One

Andrea and her father had been out in the bay cruising on their 40' Bluewater cabin cruiser almost four hours. They were thoroughly enjoying the beautiful and unusually mild June day on the boat that he'd finally bought over seven years ago. He had been preparing for his long-time dream to take many leisurely cruises with Andrea's mother on a boat large enough to live aboard. They'd always had a rather nice boat, ever since they'd bought the cottage while Andrea was still quite young, but none had ever compared to this one that gave them the luxury he'd wanted.

Her parents had dearly loved the water and had spent every weekend for years in the small inlet town. Her dad had done very well in his brokerage firm, her mother had been the manager of a very popular Bridal Shoppe for quite a few years, and they had both gotten a rather substantial inheritance from their parents' estates. After Andrea had gone off to college, they'd decided to retire early, sell their home in the city and move to the cottage permanently. He had been elated when he got to take his high school sweetheart on two fabulous cruises, one for three months and the other for four months. They'd been so excited two years ago as they were making plans for an Intracoastal cruise when her back had started hurting and they'd gone to the emergency room in a nearby city. Just days after seeing the doctor, her untimely death had occurred from a rare reaction to the medication that had been prescribed.

Being an only child, Andrea had moved to the cottage, at her father's request, after the death of her mother. Her parents had almost given up hope of having a child when she finally came along, and she had been very close to both of them. She'd been living in New York City for a year, after graduating from college. Like most young people, she'd wanted to declare her independence.

It was almost noon when Andrea had suggested that she and her dad get ready to anchor and enjoy their lunch. Her dad, who was at the wheel, had pulled into a shallow cove and she had just dropped anchor when he suddenly slumped and fell to the deck. He'd whispered, "See Cory soon," just before he was gone.

Andrea cried, "Dad, don't you leave me, too," as she administered CPR, which she knew well, but to no avail. She'd radioed for help immediately, but their services also proved futile. Her wonderful father was gone, and she was definitely alone.

She'd gotten a job at the bank when she'd come here to be with her dad, but now she will inherit the lakeside cottage, the boat, and the rest of her dad's estate when his Will is probated. She'd always loved the little town and the cottage, but she isn't quite sure it's where she wants to spend the rest of her life. She knows very few people, as she had come only on weekends before she'd left for college, and most of the friends she'd made during those years are probably no longer around. At least, she hadn't seen any of them at the bank and she'd spent most evenings with her dad. She'd also felt that her co-workers were quite a bit older or married so that hadn't produced any close friends, male or female. However, she is now thankful for her job because it has kept her mind occupied with other things besides her sorrow.

It has been over two months, and Andrea knows she has really been putting off the inevitable—the reading of her father's Will, but it's a task she hasn't felt she could handle yet. She had been especially close to her father since her mother passed away, and the thought of facing the final steps of closing his estate had been something that had always sent shivers up her spine. With no one to share her sorrow, the loss of her dad had been almost more than she could accept, let alone having to talk to a stranger about his money, his wishes, and his bequeaths. It just seemed so impersonal.

So, she'd been avoiding going to the attorney, even though her father had told her the office was right here in town and he'd made sure everything was in order. He'd even tried several times to arrange meetings for her to meet this young attorney, but that had never happened. Of course, she keeps remembering his final words to her, "See Cory soon."

What is really bothering her now, though, is the visit from this rather weird guy, a Clayton Rogers, who had moved into a large exotic house up on the hill shortly after her father's death. It had been standing empty for a year or more, and it had always reminded her of one you might see as a haunted house around Halloween. She'd often wondered what he did for furniture because she had never seen any being moved in.

He'd come to her door one night, about a week ago, and had rather forcefully invited himself in. He'd talked about a chest that her father owned, and he'd offered to buy it since he was certain she wouldn't have any use for it. She had never actually seen the chest, but her father had told her and her mom about finding one quite a few years ago. He'd said that he was saving it for their retirement. How this guy knew about it was certainly a mystery, but she'd told him she had no idea of its whereabouts. She had somehow convinced him to leave, but he said he'd be back because he was going to find that chest.

*Well, I suppose I should contact this attorney Dad designated,* she ponders as she is now trying to convince herself that it is time. *It just seems rather strange, though, because Dad had done business for years with the same law firm up in Boston. He just told me that the attorney, with whom he'd been doing business, retired so he'd decided to find one closer to the cottage. I hadn't even known there was an attorney in this little town, but I guess with one of my vacations starting tomorrow, I'd better call and make an appointment with this Cory Calhoun. Hopefully I can struggle through one more ordeal. I do want to see if there is something I can do about this weirdo who says he's going to find that chest.*

She'd gotten up early Monday morning and quickly called his office before she could change her mind again. They'd had an opening at 10:30, so she's now almost to the office door, her heart in her throat. She'd walked the few blocks from the cottage to the office, hoping to prolong the time before she was faced with the agony of hearing the contents of the last legal papers her dad had prepared. As she started to enter, another client was just leaving so she assumed her appointment would be the next one. She noted that the firm apparently consists of only the one lawyer and his secretary. It's a very nice building right on the Main Street and definitely closer for her than making a trip to Boston. The nice appearing lady, she would guess, is most likely in her late fifties and has a pleasant and welcoming smile.

"Good morning, Miss Harrington," she welcomed as Andrea entered and approached the desk. Andrea wondered how she knew her name, but quickly realized she'd just made the appointment so she could most likely assume who she was.

She thought, however, as she glanced around the office, *They must not have too many clients if they can assume who everyone is when they come in the door.*

Andrea looked toward the desk again when she heard, "You may take a seat if you'd like, but Mr. Calhoun will be with you shortly," the secretary continued. "We are really quite anxious to handle your father's estate and appreciate your promptness this morning."

A door soon opened to one of four private offices, which were located off a central hall leading to what appeared to be a large conference room across the back of the building. Andrea found herself staring at a tall, dark and handsome young man who looked just a few years older than she, maybe around 30. He had the most captivating smile on his face as he came toward her. "Good morning, Miss Harrington, it's so nice to finally meet you. Your father had told me that you were a lovely person, but I see he could have added a few more adjectives. Please come in."

He had actually seen just a glimpse of her at the funeral, but in black and her sorrow and tears so prevalent, it had been far from a true picture of the beauty he sees today. He now extends his hand to her, as he held the door with his back so she could enter, but he didn't let go as he led her to a chair. He had glanced at Donna, his secretary, and mouthed, "Wow!"

Andrea wasn't sure if she could make it to the chair he was holding for her. The sudden warmth of his hand on hers had emotions going clear down to her toes. In fact, she wasn't sure if she could concentrate on any business with him in the same room. *I wonder if my father had any idea what kind of an impression this Cory Calhoun would have on me.*

"Oh, I . . . I'm sorry," she stammered, "did I . . . I miss something you said? My mind is sort of playing tricks on me today since this is something I haven't looked forward to."

"I had just remarked that your father was an exceptional man, Andrea, as you must already know. But you're not aware, I'm pretty sure, that he was also like a father to me—a hero I'll always treasure because I'd never had my father when I was growing up. He died when I was three years old, so I don't remember much about him except for the pictures and stories my mother has told me. My sister is three years older than I and still lives with our mother. Being an author, she can do her work at home so has been a great companion to our mother after graduating from college.

But, this meeting is about your father and his Last Will and Testament. It was during my last year of Law School when your father came to our class and asked the Professor if he could interview three or four of the top students. After the top ten had been identified, your father obtained the records of eight and had the Professor point them out to him. After the first meeting, he selected four and met with us at our convenience. He then asked me to meet with him again, and it was then that he asked if I would be willing to work with him on a special project. I don't know how much he confided in you, but he asked me to give you all the details when I thought you should or would want to know.

One thing I do think you should know right away, Andrea, is the fact your father knew he was dying. Approximately five years before your mother's death, not too long after you had started college, I believe, he had been diagnosed with a rare heart problem, and that is why he retired, bought the boat, and was determined that your mother would have at least one cruise with him before it was too late. He felt so very blessed when they got to take the second one, and he'd so wanted to take her on that Intracoastal trip they were planning. She had been so happy working out all the details. It was such a tragedy that he had to lose her because those cruises really seemed to be what both of them had dreamed about for years."

"How—ah—how do you know all this? Why didn't he tell me? I've been here for him the last two years! Do you think he ever told my mother?" she said in anguish.

"Andrea, please don't feel he was shutting out you or your mother. It wasn't at all like that. He just wanted to protect both of you from the worry of knowing it could happen, but not knowing when or where it would be. He wanted to live a normal family life without being watched constantly for fear of something happening. Can't you just be happy that he was able to do what he loved and with the only love of his life that he had left? I understand the two of you took a very nice cruise last year, too."

"Yes, we did, but he told you all this and you were a complete stranger." She knew she was being difficult, but she couldn't hold back her tears as she realized that her dad had told all this to his attorney but hadn't confided in his very own family. "I'd always thought that we'd shared everything," she said still rather emotionally as all this new information was causing her to tremble. She took a minute to calm her nerves and then said in a steady voice. "He told me his attorney in Boston had retired, and now it turns out it was you all along?"

"One of the older men with whom he'd worked on financial strategy for years did retire from a Boston firm. He'd informed me of the retirement when we'd met several times before I graduated and went to work for the same Law Firm in Boston. It was mostly just discussing a series of questions concerning my opinion on this or that, but he did mention a special project he was working on but not quite ready to put it in legal form. This firm approached me about a job, just before the end of the term, so it could've been on his recommendation although he never mentioned it," he chuckled. "He came to see me quite often then, about five years ago, as he made decisions on how everything would be handled upon his death and also started putting me in charge of his other financial interests, too. It was right after your mother died that he came and asked if I would consider opening a small office here if he would provide the building and also guarantee a certain monthly income.

He had wanted you to know his former attorney in Boston had retired and he'd decided to find one a little closer to home. I didn't quite understand that reasoning, but I assumed he didn't want you to think you could still go to that firm even though he'd told you about me who was right here. An attorney, at times, has some special privileges, I guess, but we are also put in some very difficult situations. My heart was broken when I heard of your father's death, because, as I've told you, he had become a father figure to me. I couldn't, I know, even start to feel the loss that you must have felt. However, he did make sure I would be close by when you needed the attorney to see that his wishes were fulfilled. So, here I am and we have a Last Will and Testament to read and abide by."

"Yes, I guess we'd better get to it. I hope there aren't too many more surprises that he just wanted to protect me from."

"I know that the Will I prepared for him is very straightforward. However, one day he walked in with a sealed envelope, informed me that he had made a codicil to his Will, and I was to acknowledge all the contents of the envelope as part of his Last Will and Testament. It was to override anything in the original Will that referred to the same article.

He asked if my secretary, Donna, could type a document to verify that statement, and he signed both the typed document and the envelope in front of the two of us. I have no idea what it pertains to."

He then handed Andrea the sealed envelope and the document, which she immediately could recognize as her father's own signature.

Cory unfolded the Last Will and Testament of Randall T. Harrington and began reading the contents which were no surprise to Andrea until it stated that a Trust Fund had been established in her name for $2,000,000, from which the interest could be for her use until her 35th birthday. At that time, it would be hers to do with as she chose, such as providing the schooling for her children, renovating the cottage or whatever she wanted at that time of her life. His personal worth, of course, would be available to her immediately, after all the final indebtedness and bequeaths had been satisfied.

All that had been calculated by Cory, of course, taking into consideration all his Life Insurance policies, a few sizable investments, the value of the cottage and the boat, two very sizable savings accounts, several CD Certificates, plus the personal checking account. It was a staggering $32,535,890.57. He had requested that donations be made to the church and his few favorite charities, and that Andrea retain the cottage and boat for at least five years. Needless to say, she was absolutely dumbfounded.

"Where did he get all that?" she asked. "I know he did well in business, but I didn't expect it to be more than $5,000,000 tops. Well, I know Dad and Mom both inherited some money from their parents, but I never knew how much that was."

"Did he ever mention a chest that he'd found a couple or three years after you'd started coming to the cottage? He told me that he was out fishing in the small boat you had then and his hook caught on something that he couldn't pull up. He'd decided to dive down and see what the snag was and discovered this small chest. It seems that he realized right away the value of that chest and took it into New York City to have it and the contents appraised. He'd apparently read about a pirate ship capsizing many years ago around here and all the cargo had been accounted for except one small chest.

He was awarded over $4,000,000 for finding it and turning it in. At that time, he had opened trust funds for you and your mother with half the money, but when she died, he then transferred her fund over to yours along with a tidy sum of interest that had accumulated. He'd also invested his portion, and with the interest that accumulated over the years, plus the sale of the business and home, and his other investments, he was a very rich man. He would've had a lot more, but he was also a very generous person."

"Wow," was all Andrea could say for a few seconds. "Dad did mention the chest to Mom and me, but not the amount he'd received for it."

"Well, shall we see what his codicil does to something we have just absorbed?"

"It can't be any more surprising than what I've already learned."

Giving her the most adorable smile, with just a hint of a dimple in one cheek, he slit the envelope while tingles were going up her spine like she'd never felt before. He then pulled out a sheet of stationery which she readily recognized as coming from her father's desk. He'd had that type of engraved stationery in his desk for as long as she could remember.

Cory was scanning the hand written codicil quickly before he would read it to her, but his face turned so pale she thought he was going to faint. "What is it?" she asked. "You look extremely shocked. It can't be that bad, can it? Did he decide to leave me a penniless pauper, after all?"

Shaking his head negatively, he handed the paper to her. "You'd better read it yourself, Andrea, because I can't believe it."

Andrea took the codicil and read:

To Cory Calhoun, who I consider the son I never had, and to Andrea, my lovely daughter, my one and only love since her mother left us to be with our Lord, I hereby change my official Last Will and Testament to read:

1. Cory Calhoun is to receive $4,500,000 from my personal worth for all the considerations he has shown me over the last few years.

2. Cory Calhoun is to become the owner of the 40' Bluewater Cruiser that is moored at the cottage which will now be owned by my only daughter, Andrea. The title has been transferred to his name and can be found in my desk. The boat can continue to be moored at that location, as long as it remains in Cory's

name and the cottage in Andrea's. I'm hoping the two
persons involved will find great pleasure one day using
the boat and the cottage together as man and wife.

I selected you, Cory, because I saw the qualities in you
that I felt would make my daughter's future happy and
secure. Nothing would give me greater pleasure than
to look down from above and see happiness and love
abounding again where I had them so abundantly.

3.  This may be a little premature, since I assume you are
    just meeting, but please take time to get to know each
    other, and I pray you will see in each other what I have
    seen in each of you.

Signed this 15th day of April, 2005.

S/Randall T. Harrington

They just sat and looked at each other for a few seconds
that seemed like an hour, and then Andrea started laughing.
"My father playing matchmaker—I would've never guessed
that he had that ability.

Well, Mr. Calhoun, it appears you have come into a nice
sum of money and also a boat that I thought would be mine.
My father apparently had his reasons for these actions, and I'll
accept them as his final wishes. I guess he knew I'd be able to
buy another boat if I wanted to do so. As far as his mention
of sharing this boat and getting acquainted is concerned,
however, I think he went a little overboard on that request.
The boat will be there whenever you wish to use it, and if I

can help you learn the techniques of handling it, I'll be happy to do that.

If that's all for today, I'll say goodbye now." She slowly got up from the chair to leave, although feeling somewhat perplexed.

"Please wait a minute, Andrea. It looks as if your dad went to an awful lot of work to see that we got a chance to meet each other, so why don't we humor him up there and take some time to get acquainted? I'm not saying that we'd have to immediately start dating or anything, but we could be friends. I don't know very many people here, especially ones my own age, and I would welcome having a friend to do things with now and then. So, what do you think? Could you tolerate me enough to try to be my friend?"

*Could I tolerate him, he asks? I'm afraid I'd want much more than friendship if I were around him too often. He's the most handsome and tempting man I've ever seen, but he only wants to be my friend.* Aloud she could only manage to squeak out, "I can try that," as she headed for the door, but then suddenly turned back again.

Clearing her throat so her voice is now under control, she said, "There is something else I was going to talk to you about, Mr. Calhoun. There's this man who recently moved into that house up on the hill. He came around a little over a week ago asking about that chest. Apparently he isn't aware that Dad got rid of it quite a few years ago. He wouldn't take my word for it and says he's going to find it if he has to search the entire house. I was wondering if you'd have any suggestions on how

I can convince him that it is gone. It's a little weird and even scary to think he'll walk into my house anytime he wants."

Glancing at his watch, he looked concerned as he said, "Of all days, I have a client coming in shortly and another one mid-afternoon, but would you mind if I dropped over to discuss this matter with you after dinner, maybe? I definitely think something should be done before it gets out of hand."

"Well," she said a little hesitantly, "if you don't have any plans for your evening meal, we could possibly make it a dinner meeting. I love to cook and it isn't much fun cooking for just one. We can consider it as new friends getting acquainted." She couldn't keep the smile from spreading across her face.

"Tell me the time and I'll be there, Andrea. It sounds great as I'm getting pretty tired of my feeble attempts at cooking, and restaurant eating alone really gets to be a drag after a very short time," he chuckled.

"Do you think you could be there around 6:00?"

"I'll definitely be there by 6:00."

When Andrea had left the building, Cory couldn't wait to talk to Donna about the girl he'd almost let get away. "How could I have been so arrogant, Donna, to turn down invitation after invitation from that wonderful man who just wanted me to meet his lovely daughter? He knew I'd fall in love with her and relieve his worries about her future, but he never put any pressure on me.

Well, I'm going to get my foot in the door this evening because she just invited me to dinner, although it's actually sort of a business meeting. This weirdo that we've seen around town the last couple of months called on her and wanted to buy a chest her father had found years ago. She asked for some help in getting rid of him."

"That weirdo we've seen around here would cause anyone to run for help, but please watch your step, Cory. After all, you've just met the girl, and you know that looks aren't everything."

"Donna, you haven't the slightest idea what my heart was doing from the moment I saw her, and I'm going to rely on my heart to tell me who I want to spend the rest of my life with. Also, Mr. Harrington wants this to happen and he picked me especially to take care of his only daughter so he can look down from heaven and see love, love, and more love in that cottage. You know he wouldn't steer me wrong, and I've never felt like this before, so I'm not wasting any time in getting acquainted with her. By the way, I am now the proud owner of the Bluewater, so maybe I can find a way to use that to get closer to her."

"Congratulations, Cory, what a fabulous gift! He must've really thought highly of you.

If you're determined to proceed with this idea of yours to satisfy Mr. Harrington as well as your own heart, I'll keep you in my prayers," she laughed.

>>                                                                      >>

*Chapter Two*

Although she had walked slowly *to* the attorney's office, Andrea couldn't keep from almost running back home. She wanted time to make sure everything was perfect when Cory showed up for dinner. She couldn't believe there was a man anywhere around who was so perfectly put together, let alone in this little town in Massachusetts. *How could my dad have persuaded him to come here when he'd been with such a prominent law firm in Boston? It's sure a mystery that I want the answer to. He'd said my dad had guaranteed him a salary and had provided the building, but could that compensate for a position in a flourishing law firm in Boston? Oh, I wonder if that means I'm obligated to continue paying him a salary. Maybe he will just return to Boston when he finishes with Dad's Will being probated and settled.*

She had just passed the Deli when she stopped, backtracked, and went in to get a quick sandwich so she wouldn't have to fix herself one at home. When she got to the cottage, she picked up the newspaper and a few other items lying around, did a quick dust job and ran the dust mop over the wooden floors. She then checked the kitchen to see if she needed to make a trip to the store. After jotting down a short list, she hurried to the grocery and also stopped at the florist shop. She wanted flowers on the table, and her flower garden was showing signs of neglect with the August heat wave they were having.

Back home, she turned on the radio and sang along with the music being played while she started fixing potato salad and also a toss salad for dinner. She'd decided to have steaks on the grill so she put some marinade on them and would do the grilling after Cory arrived. She shivered at the thought of him being in her house and cooking for him. *What was I thinking when I asked him to come for dinner? Will I actually be able to sit and look at him across the table and remain calm and able to talk? Come on, Andrea, he's just a man and you have dated a few rather handsome men before. I'll just talk to him like I used to talk to my dad—they must have some common interests since they've known each other for several years.*

She had the table set and everything else seemed to be under control, so she went to her bedroom to shower and change into fresh clothes. As she was just starting to brush her long, slightly wavy blonde hair away from her face and fasten it with a clip in the back, she thought she'd heard the front door open and shut. *Surely Cory wouldn't just walk in without even knocking first, would he? He didn't appear to be that forward when I met him this morning.*

What she hadn't expected to encounter, though, when she went toward the front door, was that weird Clayton Rogers with his long shaggy hair, beard, and clothes that resembled a vagabond, already in the living room. He seemed to be making himself at home on her couch and giving her a big smile when she couldn't help but stare at him.

"What are you doing in my house?" she asked rather disturbed and angry although she was shaking with a sort of fear she had never felt before, especially in a town that had always been so peaceful. It consisted mostly of retired people who just wanted to be near the water—a town where no one locked their doors and everyone respected the privacy of the others.

"Waitin' for you, Sweetheart," he almost drooled down his beard as he ogled her with big brown eyes that actually sparkled as the afternoon sun drifted into the room and shone on his face. They were rather fascinating and they seemed to hold her attention even though she wanted him out of her house.

"I want you out of here, Mr. Rogers. You have no right coming into my house, or any other house in this town, uninvited and acting like you actually belong. Now, please leave."

"Not until I have my say, Gorgeous One. I've come to ask you to marry me." He got down on his knees and continued, "I've been watchin' you for over three weeks now, so I know you don't have a beau. You came here to take care of your dad, and all you do is work at the bank and then come home. It must be awful lonesome for a beautiful lady like you, so I'm ready to make you my own and change your life so you'll be a happy little wife and also a mama. When do you want to get hitched, Darlin? You just set the date."

If she hadn't been so scared, Andrea would've probably laughed in his face, but she could do nothing but gasp and stare. *Why should all this be happening to me in the same day? Meeting Cory this morning had been extraordinary, but there isn't even a word to describe this—this thing. What am I going to do with him? Cory will be coming any minute and I don't want him confronting this character before we have at least a chance to discuss the situation and get a little more acquainted. Maybe I can stall before giving an answer and get him to leave for now.*

"I'm sorry, but I can't give you an answer to such an important question right now when I have company coming for dinner in just a few minutes. Would you please leave now and let me think about all you've said?"

He scrambled to his feet and ambled over to her. He grabbed her then, before she knew his intentions, and smacked his lips against hers—reminding her of a horse opening its big mouth and showing its teeth. She pulled away quickly and tried to smile as she held the door. As he almost danced down the steps, she saw a car turning the corner and was sure Cory was on his way. She raced to the bathroom, splashed her face with water and quickly used some mouth wash to try to get rid of any trace of one Clayton Rogers.

Luckily that car had not been Cory's, but another was at the corner when she got back to the door and this one, a rather late-model sports car, turned into her drive. *I wonder if that was a gift from Dad, too.* She couldn't help being a little curious as the boat situation was still fresh on her mind. She ran to the kitchen and got the tray of appetizers she'd fixed, and when she placed it on the coffee table, she realized she was shaking uncontrollably. Was it because of that Clayton, or the boat, or was it because Cory was on the doorstep? She only knew her heart was thumping very rapidly as she went to open the door and invite him in.

"Hi, Andrea," he greeted her. "It was really nice of you to invite me for dinner when it's really a business meeting. I hope you didn't go to too much trouble, but I'm sure thrilled to be here."

"It's no trouble, Mr. Calhoun. As I told you this morning, I love cooking and it's so nice to cook for two again. Dad was an easy person to cook for, but he liked things to be set properly on the table and not as an afterthought. Come on in and have some appetizers and I'll get us something to drink. I hope you'll enjoy yourself."

"I'm sure I will, Andrea, but will you please call me Cory and consider me a friend? You seem a little nervous. Is it my intrusion into your life, or is something else bothering you? I thought I saw a rather unkempt man skipping along the street as I was driving here. Did you have another visit from this Clayton Rogers, by any chance?"

Andrea had started for the kitchen, but stopped and turned to face him. "Oh, Mr.—ah, Cory, I was hoping I could handle this by myself, but I am so scared. Yes, he was here. In fact, I was in my bedroom when I heard the door open and shut. I didn't think you would just walk right in, but I was never so shocked as when I looked in here and saw him sitting on the couch as if he thought he belonged here. I couldn't believe it. And, you'd never guess what he came for—he asked me to marry him! What am I going to do?" she asked as tears filled her eyes and spilled over to run down her cheeks. She tried to wipe them away with the back of her hand, but Cory was immediately holding her in his arms, comforting her, and offering his handkerchief.

"If only I'd been a few minutes earlier and could have confronted him. I'm so sorry you had to face him again by yourself, but I intend to see that it doesn't happen again."

"And just how do you expect to do that, ah, Cory, since he doesn't seem to have any pattern of his comings and goings?" Smiling and sniffing, she moved away from him and again started for the kitchen, but he was following only a few steps behind her.

"Remember I'm your friend, Andrea, and I'm not going to let you out of my sight," he proclaimed as one trying to desperately be in charge.

There was that fantastic smile again that she had seen this morning, and her hands could hardly stay at her side. She just wanted to touch his face and maybe even taste those tempting lips, but she quickly moved to open the refrigerator door and get the pitcher of iced tea. *Get a grip,* she chided herself. "Shall we go enjoy the snacks?" she asked aloud. "If you'll carry the pitcher, I'll get the glasses and put some ice in them."

"I think I can handle that. Does this happen to be sweetened tea or should I ask if you'd have some sugar and a spoon?"

"Oh, you're one of those who needs a lot of sugar to sweeten your disposition, huh? I'll get the sugar and some lemon slices, too, just so you don't get too sweet," she laughed as she headed for the cupboard.

The evening was exciting as they easily talked about her parents, his mother and sister, and, of course, Clayton. Then the surprise codicil was mentioned and she asked if he'd like to see his boat. Of course, he was anxious to see the interior and they ended up going for a ride. It started as a short one but ended up lasting over two hours since she had given him the chance to be at the wheel. "Time flies when you're having the time of your life, right?" he asked as he backed away from the wheel and motioned for her to bring it into the dock. "I'll need a lot of practice before I attempt to dock it, especially since it is now pretty dark. I hope you're still agreeable to showing me all I need to know about owning a beautiful boat like this."

"I'll be happy to do that, Cory, but we probably should make some sort of a schedule so we'll be free at the same time."

"That isn't too hard with my light schedule, so I could, or maybe I should, try to be with you every night to protect you from the admirer who doesn't seem to make appointments like a gentleman should."

It wasn't hard, of course, for Andrea to know to whom he was referring, but she was hoping she wouldn't need protection. *I really would love to get to know him better, but how could I possibly spend every night with him and still remain just friends? But that's what he had insinuated this morning, and I'm not about to throw myself at a man, no matter what my dad wanted.*

Cory had glanced to see how she might have taken his suggestion of protecting her each and every night, but she seemed to have a puzzling look on her face. He was certainly a little disappointed because tonight had made him a little more aware of what her father had said in his codicil about their becoming friends and wanting it to lead to a happy marriage. For the first time in his life, the idea of being a husband and a father gave him a warm feeling inside that he liked very much. He knew it was awfully soon, but his heart was sending very strong sensations that he'd never felt before.

Andrea realized he was waiting for a reply from her so she tried to be non-committing as she said, "That would be a little too much to ask of you, Cory, but the next two months are a wonderful time of year to take advantage of a boat before it has to be put up for the winter. I'm pretty flexible, so let's just see how things go. Check with me when you have some free time and we'll spend it enjoying the boat and getting you trained so you can feel really confident at the wheel." She didn't notice the smug smile on his face as he had turned to get off and secure the lines.

## Chapter Three

Andrea had decided to sleep in Tuesday morning and was thoroughly enjoying the laziness she felt entitled to, but about 10 o'clock the phone started ringing. She grumbled loudly as she struggled out of the covers and reached for the phone. "Hello, this is Andrea, how may I help you?" She really hadn't wanted to say that, but it had become almost an automatic answer from her work at the bank.

"I was wondering why you wasn't at the bank today, My Little Bride-to-Be," came a voice she recognized immediately as one she'd wished she would never have to hear again. "Your company last night didn't make you sick, did he? Well, he won't have to come around anymore after we get hitched because I'll be takin' up all your time. Have you made up your mind when the weddin' is going to be, Gorgeous One?"

"Mr. Rogers, I don't appreciate your intruding on my privacy, and I want you to stop coming to my house and calling me on the phone. I'm really not interested in getting myself married to anyone, and it is none of your business why I am not at the bank today. Please just leave me alone."

"Oh, but Sweetie, we're gonna get married so I can't stop comin' to your house. That's where you are and I've gotta be with you so we can look for that chest. I've been wonderin' if it could be on that boat since you said you hadn't seen it around the house. I think your papa must've found a real good hidin' place around there somewhere, but we'll find it together, just as soon as we get hitched."

"The chest is not around here, Mr. Rogers, and I've been told that my father took it into New York City several years ago. I have no idea what happened to it."

"You're lyin' to me now, Girl," his voice rising and sounding angry, "and I don't like people lyin' to me. I never saw your father take that chest away from the cottage, and I'm sure I would've seen that. You just want me to give up lookin' for the chest so you can find it and claim it for yourself, but it should've always belonged to me."

"Why do you say it should've belonged to you?" she asked as she realized just how determined he was about finding that chest.

"I was lookin' for that chest for more than three years before you people even moved here. I knew it was around here somewhere because I'd read all about the loss of one small chest in a shipwreck. I gave up a lot to come here and almost drag the cove lookin' for it. But then, your father, the lucky S-O-G, (sonofagun) just happened to drop his hook in the exact place it was sittin'. It should've been mine, and I'm gonna find it and claim my fortune. I may have to tear your cottage and even that pretty boat apart, but I'm gonna find that chest." Before she could respond, he'd hung up.

How serious that threat was, she wasn't sure, but he sounded determined enough to make her want some advice quickly. She dialed Cory's number and was surprised to hear his voice instead of his secretary's. "Calhoun Law Firm, Cory speaking. May I help you?"

"I certainly hope so, Cory. This is Andrea and I just had the most disconcerting phone call from that weirdo. He has threatened to tear the cottage and the boat apart, if need be, to find that chest and claim his fortune."

"I'm sorry, Andrea. I'm on my way. I'll be there in about 5 minutes, if not sooner."

It is a small town, but how he got there in 3 minutes, Andrea had no idea. He came running from his car with a sack in his hand, and he sighed in relief when he saw her and knew she was unhurt. He couldn't stop himself from giving her a quick hug as he said, "I was so afraid he might beat me getting here."

She looked a bit surprised as she glanced down at the sack. "Oh, I bought these this morning before I went to the office. I was planning to come over tonight to see if you'd let me install them on your doors. They're dead bolt locks, and they said at the hardware store that quite a few families have started using them because of everything that is happening around the country these days. I've been reading reports of quite a few burglaries lately in some of the neighboring towns, and I guess our little town isn't as safe as it once was. So, since you're home today and I have no appointments, we'll just get busy and make your home a little safer if that's OK with you."

He then glanced at her as if he were seeing her for the first time, his eyes traveling from her rumpled hair down to the fuzzy house slippers and back to her face. He couldn't hold back a chuckle as he remarked, "You've had a pretty busy morning, haven't you, Kiddo? Do you know you're still in your night gown?"

She could only gasp as she looked down at herself and tried to cover her breasts and stomach with her arms and hands. Her gown was old and thin, and she realized she hadn't even put her robe on when she'd answered the phone and then called Cory. "Oh," she cried as she turned and ran toward her bedroom.

Continuing to chuckle, he called to her, "I'll go to the car and get my tools while you make yourself even lovelier than you already are. Take your time—I'm in no hurry."

When he came back into the house, he heard the shower running so he went on to the kitchen and started some coffee. He was thinking that apparently she'd been sleeping late on her vacation and hadn't even had breakfast although it's after 11 o'clock now. That means that Rogers must've called while she was still in bed. He was smiling as he wished he hadn't called attention to her type of attire quite so soon. The gown was thin and he'd gotten a pretty good look at the silhouette of that gorgeous body as she'd scampered to her room. What he couldn't quite understand was how he had missed all that when he'd first come into the house. He must have really been upset.

A few minutes later, she came into the kitchen wearing a pair of khaki pants, a cute raspberry colored top, and an embarrassed look on her face. He knew he was staring, but he couldn't help himself. She was beautiful with that wavy blonde hair, pretty blue eyes, a gorgeous complexion, and just the right curves. She went over to the coffee pot, inhaled the aroma, and poured herself a cup of the hot brew. After taking a sip, she turned toward him and smiled, "You make a good cup of coffee, Mr. Calhoun, and I thank you. This certainly hasn't been a good day so far, but I'm sure this coffee will help." Glancing at her watch, she quickly looked at him, checked the clock on the wall, but all she could utter was, "Is that really the right time?"

"I think so, but do you want some breakfast first or are you going straight to lunch? I'll be glad to go and get us some sandwiches, if you'd like that."

"Oh, no, that's all right. I'll have some peanut butter and jelly on toast, some fruit and some chips, and I'll be fine until evening. But, what can I fix you, Cory? I have makings for a Reuben or a smoked turkey sandwich. Would you like one of those?"

"Actually, I'd like to join you with the peanut butter and jelly on toast, if it's not too much trouble. If you have enough chips and fruit, I'll have some of those, too, but I hate to be eating your food again today after that delicious meal last night."

"It's no problem," she grinned, "and you're going to pay for it by installing those dead bolt locks on my doors. That's just for the labor, though. I'm going to pay you for the locks themselves."

"I'm sorry, Little Lady, but you're not paying for any locks or labor. I'm just trying to safeguard my new found friend." *And hopefully more than a friend,* he thought to himself.

Andrea was amazed that an attorney knew how to use tools at all, but he had three of those locks installed quickly, and they worked, too. He'd taken his sport jacket off, and she'd stood admiring his muscles flexing under his snug knit shirt as he was drilling the holes in the doors and sash and putting all the pieces together where they belonged. And then that smile he'd given her, when she'd congratulated him on a job well done, was enough to start her heart beating like a drum. *Remember he's just a friend,* she reminded herself.

While swishing his hands together and flexing those muscles in his upper arms to indicate he was finished, he said, "With that job done, would it be time to take a little boat ride or do you have other plans for the day?"

"I'd love that. How about taking some snacks along and maybe we can anchor out and enjoy a break before coming back in?"

"You have the greatest ideas. Can I go and pick up something?"

"No, I have some things I'll put in a basket that we can have on the boat, and then I'll let you take me out for a nice meal this evening. How's that sound?"

"It sounds like I've found a friend who is going to turn my former dull life into a very exciting one, and I love it."

The windows had locks on them although they'd never been used as far as she knew. It was sort of fun to lock up the house completely, check to make sure his car was locked, and then head for the boat. She watched as he proceeded to do all the things she had shown him last night, and he didn't miss a beat. All he has left to learn, it seems, is the docking. She's so proud of him because he was really a fast learner, and she wishes she could give him a big hug. *I must remember, however, that we are only friends.*

It was after 4 o'clock when they were going to anchor and enjoy their snacks, but then they noticed some threatening dark clouds forming in the West as if a bad storm could possibly be on its way. She thought Cory was acting a little apprehensive as he watched the dark shadows appear on the water. She'd told him earlier she was going to let him dock, so she suggested instead of anchoring out that they get docked and then enjoy their snacks on the boat, or even in the house, just in case the rain did decide to come down with force.

She wasn't surprised when he asked if she would do the docking as he didn't feel skilled enough to chance it, especially since the clouds were getting darker, the wind had increased, and he hadn't had his lesson yet on docking. He concealed a big smile by kissing her on the cheek while he murmured, "Thank you for letting me off the hook today. Those clouds bother me just a little, and I really need to concentrate if I'm going to learn how to dock this boat."

The storm had turned out to be just a gentle shower that had blown over quickly, so about 7 o'clock, he drove them to the one restaurant in town that he knew not only had a reputation for excellent food but also had a dance floor. Since it's Tuesday, a jukebox will be playing, but on most weekends they have a DJ or even a live band. "Will you dance with me,

Andrea?" he whispers as a slow number starts playing. Taking her in his arms, he feels as if her father is there smiling and urging him on, so he pulls her just a little closer. She actually responds as he'd hoped and he was elated. She seems so tiny, he leans his head down so they can dance cheek to cheek. He occasionally kisses the top of her head, and when she leans back a little to look up at him, he takes advantage and quickly kisses her lips. He was so pleased to see her cute smile. He doesn't want this evening to end because it feels so right.

When he finally takes her to the door, he remembers the threat that Clayton Rogers had made about tearing the cottage and the boat apart to find that chest, so he stops to take a quick look around before allowing her to go in. Even with the locks, he decided he'd better follow her inside and check around. Maybe he could even get a nice goodnight kiss. He then sensed her uneasiness, so he cautiously asked, "What is it, Andrea? Are you concerned about what that Clayton might do? I could spend the night, if you'd like. It would be just as a protector, of course, to make sure that weirdo doesn't pull anything."

"Oh, Cory, I don't think he would do anything during the night, would he? He probably plans to search during the day when I go back to the bank. I really don't want to interfere with you getting your rest, your busy office routine, or possibly you lively night life," she teased.

"You're funny, Andrea, but I'm sure your father had a good comfortable bed, so if you wouldn't object, I could crash there. I sort of have a feeling you're not completely at ease about staying here by yourself tonight. Am I right?"

"I'll admit I'm a little—well, actually quite scared of what he might try to do. When he raised his voice and accused me of lying to him, I was really worried that he might do anything he could think of to try and find that chest. I wish I knew what would appease the character so he would stop this harassment. I wonder if he has any idea what that chest was really worth. If he does, he probably wouldn't settle for any small sum. So, . . . ah, . . . as my new found friend, are you positive you wouldn't mind staying?" She started to giggle, and as she looked at him, tears welled up in her eyes. "Do you think my dad is looking down tonight and smiling?"

It was unbelievable that their thoughts were running on the same wave length. "Can you believe that I was wondering the same thing when I was holding you in my arms on the dance floor tonight? It's eerie, isn't it, that maybe your dad really did have it right that we are to become friends, and possibly even more than mere friends."

"Well, I'm not sure my dad had that quite right, but I do like the idea of a friend who loves to go boating, can install locks on doors, can dance and has a good personality."

And then neither could bring themselves to say goodnight. Cory pulled his car into the double garage with her father's Jeep Cherokee, which is now hers, of course. He made sure the doors of the house were locked, and then they'd settled down on the couch to watch a late movie.

It was somewhat later when he awoke and found Andrea asleep with her head on his shoulder. Glancing at his watch, he saw that it was 1 o'clock, the TV was still on, and he hated to move to turn it off, but he knew they'd both be more comfortable if they were in their own beds. "Andrea," he whispered, "it's time to go to bed."

"Oh," she gasped as she sat up quickly, looking aghast at finding she'd been asleep on his shoulder. "I'm sorry I didn't see much of the movie, but I'll see you in the morning," she mumbled and hastily hurried off to her room.

Grinning to himself, Cory clicked off the TV and lights and slowly made his way in the dark toward the small light Andrea had turned on in her father's bedroom earlier.

# Chapter Four

Cory had stayed Wednesday night also, but when Andrea noticed that Clayton hadn't been around on Wednesday or Thursday, after the phone call Tuesday morning, she had then told Cory that he didn't need to stay with her Thursday night. She'd even made a remark that maybe they'd scared him off as they were enjoying a wonderful Glazed Chicken and Rice Combo Friday evening in the small Chinese restaurant that had just recently opened.

"That would be so nice," Cory had replied, "but I'm not convinced that he'll give up so easily. He seems fascinated with you, wants to marry you, and he's determined to find that treasure chest. You're the apple of his eye, Andrea, and I know I wouldn't give up if I were in his shoes." His eyes sparkled as he grinned and batted his long, curly eyelashes.

"You're really too much, Mr. Calhoun, I mean Cory. Are you sure you don't wear false eyelashes just to attract attention from all the ladies?" Laughing, she continued, "They are very outstanding, I must admit. Was your sister blessed with them, too?"

"It's funny that you'd ask, because she didn't get ones as long as mine. My father was the one, apparently, who had the very long lashes, and I inherited them from him. Mom's and Sissy's are fairly long and dark, and they curl slightly, but just not quite as long as mine. I sometimes wish they were reversed because I've gotten a lot of teasing over the years because of them."

"I won't tease you about them, Cory, but they do cause my heart to pump a little faster when you flutter them at me," she giggled. "But, O.K., back to this Clayton Rogers. You're telling me that I probably have a long endurance race with him, even though we haven't seen him around now for three days. Where do you suppose he's been and what do you suppose he's been up to?"

"That's the million dollar question, I'm afraid. He doesn't seem to play according to any of the rules. I wish I had a crystal ball to look into."

Saturday and Sunday went smoothly with neither of them catching even a glimpse of the strange Clayton Rogers. They took a boat ride in the afternoon on Sunday, but he'd opted to let her dock it again because he didn't want her to think she was done with the teaching job so soon.

On Monday, Andrea had been up and ready for work early. She hadn't realized how much she'd actually missed her job and seeing the people come and go from the bank. She'd gotten in the habit of locking the doors at home when she left, however, and she did realize that it gave her a sense of security.

When Clayton started to open the door at Andrea's about 10 o'clock, however, he was just slightly surprised to see that it was locked—he'd been expecting her or the attorney to take steps to keep him out of the house. He'd made a trip into Boston on some business Tuesday, after he'd called her, so had missed that action since he'd just returned yesterday. He did sort of wonder, though, if she'd hired it done or if Cory Calhoun, her attorney, actually had the know-how to do it for her. He, himself, could've done it in the blink of an eye.

*That's all right,* he pondered and then smiled. *They probably think I've given up since they haven't seen me for several days, and they'll soon relax their guard. I've got a mission to perform, however, until I know the results are all to my liking. So, I guess I'll have to tackle the boat and see how I can be a nuisance there.*

Chuckling, he headed slowly toward the dock and that nice big boat. *It's such a shame that Andrea's dad and mom hadn't been able to enjoy it more after all the planning they'd done.*

*I had really liked and respected Mr. Harrington. I also remember being a part of that small group that included Andrea. She had come here with her folks every weekend while she was growing up, and her dad and mom had done a lot of kind things for all of the kids that Andrea got to know. I wonder how long it's going to take her to figure out who I am and what I'm up to? At least she's gotten to the attorney's office.*

It was now late afternoon and the day had been going well at the bank. Andrea had just happened to glance up toward the teller's window and couldn't believe that Clayton Rogers was standing there in line. He was looking right at her. He smiled and even waved, and she again noticed the distinctive sparkle of his eyes as she had the day he'd been in her house. She just wished she could see them up close because they remind her of someone's eyes she had been intrigued with before, but she can't remember when or where.

She immediately called Cory and informed him that their good fortune had just vanished. "At least my doors are locked so I won't have to confront him in my living room, but do you think we should check the boat right after work?"

"It wouldn't be a bad idea. I don't know what his intentions were when he said he might have to tear it apart, but I'm almost inclined to take it to the marina and have it taken out of the water and stored. Boats are a little hard to protect at private docks. I can get away in about fifteen minutes, so I think I'll drive on down there and see if anything has happened today that shouldn't have."

"I should be able to leave shortly, too, so I'll see you at the boat."

When she glanced back to the teller window, Clayton was gone and was nowhere in sight. In a fright, she checked out, headed for her dad's car and drove toward home. She was shaking as she ran down the path to the boat, but she didn't see anything amiss as she came near the stern. She was just stepping onto the dock when she heard Cory's car pull into the drive, so she waited for him to join her. Nothing seemed out of place on the outside, but when they entered the cabin, they knew someone had been there. All of the cupboard doors were open in the galley, the head door stood open, the closet doors in the forward cabin were open, and the rug was thrown back so that the bilge compartment could be searched. Nothing had been damaged, and it didn't take long to straighten up the disarray, but it was disheartening to realize someone would want to invade another person's property and leave a mess.

Cory decided right then that he was going to talk with the police chief and see if he could do something that would get this guy out of their lives. He instructed Andrea to go to the house, keep the doors locked, and he would be back as soon as he had some answers.

The Chief listened with a rather smug look on his face, and then remarked, "He is a rather amusing sort, isn't he? I really don't think he would actually damage anything—that isn't what this is all about." Immediately his face turned a brilliant red and he excused himself by saying he had an appointment he'd almost forgotten about. He hurried out the door leaving Cory to stare after him.

"What the devil did that remark mean?" Cory mumbled to himself as no one else was near. "That isn't what this is all about?" he repeated the Chief's remark aloud. "I know for sure now that something is going on here, and it looks like some kind of a set up. I'm going to pay a visit to this Clayton Rogers and try to find out what it is."

In the meantime, Andrea is wondering why she feels so certain that she has seen those sparkling brown eyes before. Talking to herself, she mumbles, "They're not a solid brown, like Cory's, but the iris has a circle of yellow around the pupil which makes them so striking, but where have I seen them before? Gosh, could it have been around here? I did spend time with kids about my own age, but you can't really tell how old this guy is." Her mind was so full of thoughts that she almost missed the phone ringing, but thinking it was Cory, she didn't hesitate to answer.

"Hey, Gorgeous One, you made it a little hard for me to search the house today, but it'll be easier after we get married. I got a good start on the boat, though. See you soon, my little Honey Bun." He hung up again before she could say a word.

"Oooh, those boys were Dean, Chuck, Bryan, Joey, Steve, Roger, and Andy. She was moaning as she tried to remember the faces of each one until she came to Roger. "That's it!

Those eyes have to belong to Roger Dayton, but why is he acting this way and going by an alias, Clayton Rogers? He was so cute and a lot of fun, he loved to ham it up and talked about his parts in the school plays, but he was very serious about becoming a Mechanical Engineer and hoping to own a company some day. He was two or three years older and went off to college shortly after his folks had disappeared on a mission trip to Africa. Could he have been hurt that much by the tragedy?"

It was getting quite late when she heard the knock, and although she realized it was most likely Cory, she cautiously checked before unlocking the door and letting him in. She wanted to tell him what she had discovered, but she could see that he had a smile on his face, so the Police Chief must have given him some hope.

"I think we'll be all right now, Andrea. The Chief was very helpful and I don't think we have anymore to worry about." He had decided not to tell her the whole story of his visit with the mystery man, since it was getting so late. He wanted to be able to give her every little detail of why all this was happening.

"That's good to hear, Cory, but he did call me again tonight. I was trying to think of the guys I'd met around here, and after his call, I finally remembered where I'd seen those eyes. Why he's going by Clayton Rogers, I have no idea, but his real name is Roger Dayton and he was in the group of kids that I hung around with on the weekends when my folks and I came here. I can't imagine why he's acting so weird unless his parents' disappearance on a mission trip really did affect him in some way. I remember that Dad spent a lot of time with him after he'd gotten the news, and then he'd gone away to college."

"The Chief didn't seem to think that he would do any real damage, but he promised to talk to him about doing anymore of this harassing." Taking her in his arms, he quietly whispered in her ear, "Could I have just a little kiss for getting a solution to our problem?"

"I thought we were only going to be friends, Mr. Calhoun. That's what you said the day we read my father's matchmaking speech." Giggling, she slipped out of his arms and curled up on the far end of the couch, but he was determined to pull her over into his arms and give her a kiss that had her toes curling in her shoes.

"If I remember correctly, your father hoped that our friendship would become a sharing of boat and cottage together as man and wife, and I'm becoming more and more in tune with his thinking."

"That would be a huge step right now, Cory, and I think I would like to take those steps we need to take very slowly. After all, we haven't even known each other a whole month yet."

"And I've known couples who were married after just a month of dating."

"But are they still together? I don't believe in going into marriage with absolutely no knowledge of one another's short comings, and when I do make that commitment, it's going to be for the rest of my life."

"You're beautiful, Andrea, and you're probably so right, but I wasn't asking for a solid commitment to marry me tomorrow, just some cuddling and some kisses every few hours," he chuckled as he snuggled his face against her neck, nibbled on her ear lobe, and slowly worked his way around to her lips.

"Men!" she moaned as she pushed him away. "You're all impossible, so before you get anymore ideas, just give me one more of those toe curling kisses and then you'd better take yourself home," she giggled.

"I am making a little dent in your armor, ain't I?" he laughed as he willingly gave her the kiss she'd asked for, and then another one, before he headed for the door. "I'll see you in my dreams, Sweetie, and definitely in person tomorrow."

>>                                                                    >>

## Chapter Five

Cory had gotten himself into bed but he couldn't sleep or even keep from smiling as he rehashed the conversation he'd had with Clayton Rogers/Roger Dayton. He'd been just a little apprehensive as he'd approached the door, but was even more startled when the door opened and a nice looking guy, about 5'11" with dark brown hair and unusual brown eyes had smiled and said, "It's about time, Cory. Come in, please. Pardon my addressing you as Cory, but I feel I know you pretty well by now." He then started laughing. "I assume, from that puzzled look you're giving me, that the Chief must've played his part well."

"What in the devil is going on? Is everyone trying to chase Andrea and me out of this town or what?"

"No, not out of town, Cory, but into each other's arms for safety, and hopefully, into a long lasting love. Andrea's father, what a saint he was, knew that his daughter was one of those strong-willed and independent individuals, and he really admired her for it—but he was also afraid she would come here to take care of him and then feel compelled to stay here all by herself after his Will was read. As you've probably noticed, there aren't many people our ages living here, so he took it upon himself to do something about her being alone. His first step was to select you and to somehow get you to open an office here. I certainly don't know how he accomplished that feat, but knowing Mr. Harrington, he was very creative in the pursuit of his goals. Are you following so far?"

Cory could only nod his head affirmatively as he remembered why he'd moved here and now waited to learn more of this perfect scheme to unfold.

"I'll have to take you back about fourteen or fifteen years now to when Andrea's father bought the cottage and started coming every weekend to enjoy the water. He fell in love with the little town almost immediately, and he saw the possibilities that it had for improvement. I think that each and every one of us, who spent time with Andrea, was checked out personally by her dad, but unknown even to Andrea. He and his wife put on great parties for us, and he was involved in so many ways that he affected all of our lives, especially mine.

You see, the summer just following my graduation from High School, my parents left on a mission trip to Africa where my mother was going to teach and Dad was to help start a medical clinic. They signed a commitment form for four years and promised to be back for my graduation from college, but they never made it to their destination. When the news came, Mr. Harrington was the first to arrive at our house and just led me through every step. He became my counselor, guide, and father image. From talking to all of us kids, he knew our dreams for the future, and he set out to help me attain the dream I had thought was down the tubes when my parents disappeared. I'd also thought he might have neglected his own brokerage firm in order to help me, but after getting to know him better, I'm sure, somehow, he managed both.

Anyway, he proceeded to help me sell the house, which covered all of my tuition, other than the first semester my folks had paid before they left, and all the other expenses for the four years. He then checked periodically to make sure I had enough spending money, plus so many other things, like helping procure my first job out of college. He also knew I loved to act, since his family had come to many of the plays that I'd been in at the High School. About six years ago, or just before he retired, he called me to his office and talked to me about this scheme of his. He entrusted me with the knowledge of his rare health situation and his Will. He'd wanted me to know why everything had to work out so that I would be willing to carry out his wishes.

At that time, he just happened to have a new secretary, which I thought was odd since he was retiring, but he just introduced us and asked if I would take her to lunch as she was rather new in town. Another little scheme of his, of course, and she is now my wife of almost four years, and she has enjoyed this episode to the fullest. Also, Mr. Harrington bought this house for us so that when the time came that I needed to be here, it would be ready, fully furnished with my wife's selections. He hoped that we would fill it with love, kids, and a lot of happiness." With a big grin, he added, "We're giving it some serious thought.

Of course, after he lost Mrs. Harrington and had you established here, he came to see me at my office and we put the final touches on my responsibility to see that Andrea would need you and, hopefully, you would take it from there. Actually, he was hoping he could get the two of you acquainted, but he could never quite accomplish that. He told me your schedule seemed pretty full for a small town attorney besides being a new kid in town. He thought you might be putting up barriers because he talked about Andrea so much, but he'd just grin and say that you'd have to meet her some day.

When he died, everything kicked into gear. I own an Engineering Firm now, again with some assistance from Mr. Harrington. I also have great personnel who can handle all the necessary activities while I'm away, so I was free to carry out the hardest acting role of my life. I hated having to scare Andrea, but I was more than satisfied when she finally ran to you as her father had hoped and planned. I must admit that I had begun to wonder if she was ever going to contact you for the reading of his Will. I wasn't supposed to do anything until she'd met you, but I finally decided to pay her a visit hoping it would get the ball rolling. I was afraid it had failed when it took over a week for her to get the appointment."

Cory was laughing, by this time, recalling his conversation with Mr. Harrington and the skilled persuasion of getting him to come to this little town, plus the never ending talk about his beautiful daughter. "He was definitely a master, and it worked. I was fully captivated by his beautiful daughter the moment I saw her, but I'm not quite sure if she's ready to return the sentiment."

"Oh, she's under your spell, Cory, don't worry about that. Actions speak louder than words, and her actions from the time she left your office that day have shown plenty of that special affection that is needed in good relationships. Let me introduce my wife." He excused himself and returned with Grace, introducing her as his co-conspirator in this charade. She was a tiny, but charming, dark-haired beauty with brown eyes that sparkled almost as bright as Roger's. "Now that I'm back to being myself, I'll be heading back to my regular job and let you finish the dreams of our dear friend, Randall Harrington. We will, however, be taking advantage of this beautiful old hide-away often, according to Grace, so hopefully we can become close friends."

"Thanks, Roger. It's good to know that my great father figure, a story I'll have to share with you sometime, was behind all this scheming even though I was ready to fight you for Andrea's love. I'm so glad you're already married so I won't have to compete with you, and I can proceed with my plans to marry the girl I now only wish I had let her dad introduce me to. I certainly hope we can have the children that her dad hopes to look down from above and see in the cottage where he says his love was abundant. That's a quote from his Will."

Cory turned over on his side and grabbed his pillow, hugging it tightly but lovingly, and went to sleep dreaming it was Andrea in his arms.

Andrea was having trouble believing that all their problems with Roger Dayton/Clayton Rogers were over just because the police chief had said so. She'd tossed and turned, she didn't know for how long, wishing Cory had stayed so she'd feel safe. *Of course, it wasn't his fault that he'd gone home. I'd pretty well set the rules when I told him the other day that he was no longer needed to stay over. If I wasn't always so darn independent, maybe guys would find me a little more appealing, and if Cory were only a little more forceful, I know I'd melt in his arms. But that isn't what I want either. I want someone who accepts me for who I am, not someone who would try to change me or my beliefs.*

She pushed herself up in bed so she was resting against the pillows and continued her thoughts. *And that reminds me—I haven't opened my Bible or even gone to church since Dad died. He really wouldn't like that as we rarely missed a Sunday service during my growing up years or since I came back to be with him. I was mad at you, God, for taking both my dad and mom away from me, but I know I have to accept your plan and go on with my life, and that has to include having You beside me.* She reached over to turn on the light, and picked up the Bible her parents had given her on her sixth birthday. She still loved it the most although she had three others she had received through the years. She read for about twenty minutes and when she slipped down under the covers, she was soon sound asleep.

When she awoke Tuesday morning, she was so relaxed, refreshed, and ready for the new day. She remembered looking at the clock while she was reading and it had been 2 a.m., so she wondered how she could feel so wide awake. Maybe getting back on the right track with God gives one a little help in all aspects of life. She couldn't help singing as she headed for the shower.

She was sitting at the kitchen table with her cup of coffee and the newspaper when the knock came on the door. She was hoping it was Cory so she could tell him that she was going to church on Sunday and ask if he would go with her. But, when she looked through the glass in the front door, she couldn't believe her eyes. Roger Dayton was standing there, not as the weird Clayton Rogers, but a grown-up, clean-cut, well-dressed handsome Roger Dayton. She pulled the door open and he smiled sheepishly as he entered, took her in his arms and gave her a little kiss. It was nothing like the horse's grin that he had used before, and it didn't even start to give her the tingles that Cory's kisses arouse, but it was nice.

"Can you forgive me?" he asked.

She pushed away from him as she asked, "What do you think you've been doing, Roger, by acting like some weird vagabond and scaring me half out of my wits? You really should be ashamed of yourself because I thought we had been friends, but it was hard to figure out who you were until I recognized your eyes. Are you trying another tactic now to find the chest, which I've told you is not around here? You look like you're sane today, so it must not be your parents' disappearance that sent you off your rocker. I just can't understand any of it, and I certainly don't know why the police chief telling Cory everything would be OK is going to make it so. I want some answers, so come into the living room and tell me what's wrong with you." She grabbed his hand and pulled him to the couch.

It was Roger's turn to be surprised now. *Didn't Cory come and explain to her what I'd been up to? How much should I tell her? Oh, why didn't Grace and I just leave town as we'd originally planned. I've really messed it up now.*

"Oh . . . . Ah, do you happen to have some coffee, Andrea? I remember your mother used to make the best coffee. Do you make it as good as she did? I thought I could smell some when I came in." He closed his eyes for a minute to pray, *Please give me time to think, Lord, before I say something I shouldn't.*

"You came here for a cup of coffee? Yes, I have a cup of coffee for you, but it may be on your head if you don't give me some answers." She turned and marched toward the kitchen, but before she got far, there was a knock on the door and Cory walked in. His expression was grim as he looked at Roger, who just shrugged his shoulders after he'd turned to see where Andrea was. She was standing with her hands on her hips and a very disgusted look on her face as she leered at one and then the other. "You two are up to something, and I doubt it has anything to do with the police chief, but one of you had better start talking before you each get a cup of coffee on your head."

She proceeded on into the kitchen, and Roger had just enough time to whisper to Cory what had happened so far before Andrea appeared with two cups of coffee.

"Oh, Honey, that coffee sure smells good," Cory said as he approached her with that cute smile he was hoping would dazzle her like it usually had.

"Don't honey me, Cory Calhoun. Until I know what has been going on around here, this coffee remains with me unless I decide to douse the two of you with it."

"O.K., come sit down and we'll tell you the story that I thought was too long to tell you last night, but can we have the coffee to wet our throats?"

After studying them for a bit, she handed each of them a cup and sat between them on the couch. They tried to tell her an abbreviated version that didn't make all of them, her dad included, horrible conspirators in the plot. Nevertheless, she was furious. She glared at each of them, got up from the couch and motioned with her hand and arm for them to get out of her house.

"Andrea," Cory begged as he and Roger headed for the door.

"Out," was all she could say without crying, and she was determined not to cry in front of two guys whom she felt had made a fool of her. She didn't even take time to grasp the fact that Cory could have been an innocent bystander, but hearing that her dad had been a part of such a scheme was just too much for her to handle right now. She'd locked the door by the time they'd reached the bottom of the steps, and then she ran to her bedroom and fell onto the bed. "How am I ever going to get over this?" she sobbed.

"Well, I guess Clayton can't help anymore, Cory, and I'm so sorry. I wish Grace and I had just taken off, but I thought I should see Andrea before I left. I thought you had most likely told her some of the story last night, but I quickly realized that you hadn't when she let me have it with both barrels. I tried to stall, by asking for coffee, so I could come up with something, but she was ready to douse me with that coffee before you came in." He couldn't help but chuckle as he continued, "That girl hasn't changed a bit since she was only twelve or thirteen, so you have your work cut out for you if you continue to pursue her. I wish I knew of something I could do to help you, but I'm afraid I did too much damage already by coming here this morning. If you need me for anything, Cory, here's my card. Give me a call."

"Thanks, Roger, and don't blame yourself for coming over to tell her goodbye. I'm the one at fault, as usual, but I'll find some way to make amends. She loves my dazzling smile and my long eyelashes, at least she did, so I'll try some cute tactics to bring her back to me. I can't lose her now because she has become too big a part of my life."

"Yep, you're in love, Cory, and I wish you all the luck in the world in taming her."

"I wouldn't want to do that, Roger, because I love her just the way she is. She has made my life so exciting, full of happiness, and she's become everything to me. I'm sure I'll think of something because I know God is with me and He'll help."

"Grace and I will be praying, too."

Cory went to the door of the cottage that evening to see if he could talk to her and try once again to apologize, but the door was locked and she would not answer his pleas or the continuous knocking. The next day, seeing her sitting at her desk, he stepped into the bank, but she immediately went into the restroom. This continued for over two weeks, his phone calls were not answered, doors remained locked, and she would not stay at her desk if he ventured into the bank.

He tried going to the boat, thinking it might lure her to come see what he was doing, but that didn't work either. He had checked all the cupboards, closets, and even the storage areas until he knew them by heart. *Why didn't I think to keep one of those keys when I was installing the deadlocks? Of course, she probably has the original lock locked, too. I have written her notes, sent flowers, a big box of chocolates, and even a Norfolk Pine, but no reply. There's only one thing left for me to do and that is to leave.*

*Chapter Six*

By Friday, the 20th of the month, he'd cleared his desk, which wasn't hard in this little town, and he then asked Donna to take messages if there were any calls. He'd explained the situation to her and said he would keep in touch.

She just smiled a little smugly and whispered, "Remember I told you beauty was only skin deep. I guess you need a lot more prayers than I thought."

"Don't give up on me and Mr. Harrington, Donna. We may not always be right, but we have persistence," he grinned as he waved goodbye. He quickly packed some casual clothes, headed for the boat, and was soon on his way to nowhere.

He called his mother and sister and asked if they would like to join him for a short cruise, so they planned to board at Quincy on his second day out. It was great seeing them, and they had a lot to catch up on, but his heart was so heavy because the only one he really wanted to be with wasn't anywhere around.

When Andrea came home from work Friday afternoon, she started to follow the routine she had laid out for herself—lock the doors, try to eat something, get ready for bed and then read or watch a movie. But right now, she wishes she could go for a boat ride because it is a beautiful day, and it would be so great being with Cory. *Yes, I miss him, and I don't think he knew what my dad and Roger were up to. He was genuinely upset with the antics of Clayton when he had to go to the Chief of Police with a complaint, and then deciding to confront the crazy Clayton all by himself who turned out to be Roger. What a ridiculous scheme, and to learn that my own father had been a part of it is really hard to grasp.*

She walked over to the window just to look at the boat and dream, but she gasped when she saw it was gone. *Where is it? Did someone cut the lines and let it float out into the Bay? Cory wouldn't try to take it out by himself, would he? How will he dock it? We never got around to lessons on docking,* she moaned. She grabbed her jacket and ran to the dock to check the cleats to see if they were okay, which they were, and then she just stood gazing out toward the channel. She wondered if she should call the Coast Guard, but then decided against that until she knew where Cory was. She ran back to the house and picked up the phone to call his office.

She heard "Calhoun Law Firm, this is Donna speaking, may I help you?"

Andrea was so choked up she could hardly talk, but she managed to ask, "Is Cory there, Donna? This is Andrea."

"I'm sorry, but Mr. Calhoun is out of the office for an indefinite period of time, Miss Harrington, and I have no way to contact him. I'm sorry," and Andrea heard a click. She had hung up on her. *Oh, Dear God, what have I done now? Wasn't*

*I ever taught that you can push a person only so far and then they'll push back? I've missed you so much, Cory, I've cried myself to sleep night after night, but I was still too stubborn to admit that I wanted to be in your arms. Now you've left me and I don't know what to do. Where could you go all by yourself when you're not that experienced with the boat? Oh, Cory, please come back.*

Cory didn't call into the office until Monday and then Donna told him that Andrea had called and sounded quite upset. After ending the call, he smiled and couldn't help thinking *she does miss me, or is it just the boat she's worried about? Well, you stubborn little imp, you can just worry a few more days because I'm not running back to you at the first sign of regret on your pretty little lips.*

He thought about how she had so diligently and unselfishly taught him the workings of the boat, even though she must have been a little disappointed that her dad hadn't left it to her in his Will. She had really been a great teacher, and it hadn't bothered him that he'd known all of it for years. It had been a way to spend time with her and get acquainted, so he'd willingly played the novice.

He had worked on a privately owned yacht over the summers during his college and law school years, and he'd actually piloted a 50 footer down the Intracoastal to Florida. *She didn't need to know that, did she? I guess that's another secret I've kept from her, though, and one she could take offense to. Oh, you've really made a botch of this relationship, you dumb attorney, and you'd better get your mind working on how you're going to straighten it all out. You need to get the one you want for your future wife back in your arms.*

After about five days his guests appeared to be getting anxious to get back home so he turned back toward the west side of the Bay. Donna had reported, when he'd called on Thursday, that Andrea had called the second time to inquire if she had heard from him and if he was having any problems with the boat. She admitted she had chuckled a little at that because she knew of his experience, but Cory hoped she had caught herself in time so that Andrea hadn't noticed.

His mother and sister got off on Saturday and he planned to dock late Sunday afternoon at the cottage. He hoped Andrea would be home and would come running into his arms, but he couldn't quiet his nerves. It would be his luck to hit the pier for the first time in his life with his hands so clammy and his whole body tense with anticipation.

Andrea had tried everything to keep from worrying about how Cory was handling the boat. *He had to get gas and surely he had stopped nights at marinas. Oh, how I wish I were with him right now. But here I am, due to my stupidity, cleaning the house, painting my bedroom walls and buying new furniture for the living room which Dad and I had been planning to do. And so far, reading a dozen or more books to make me sleepy. Even the librarian is smiling and calling me by name now.*

Sunday afternoon she opted to fix a meat loaf and have a decent meal because she'd hardly eaten since Cory left. *It wouldn't help if I were in the hospital if he decides to come back.* She went to the kitchen and started cutting onions, which only made her cry, rolled the crackers, and got out the eggs, milk and meat. She had mixed the ingredients and had just put the loaf in the baking dish when she heard a familiar sound not very far out on the water. A boat was coming into the cove, but could it be Cory? She ran to the window and couldn't hold back a scream as she quickly washed her hands, grabbed her jacket and scooted out the door to race down the path to the dock.

She was there in time to catch the lines, when he tossed them to her, and to secure the boat before she scrambled on deck and threw her arms around him. "Don't you ever do that again, Cory Calhoun, unless I'm with you. I've been so afraid, and so lonesome, and I almost went crazy because I wanted to be in your arms and kiss, kiss, kiss you," and she proceeded to do just that as he stood spellbound at such an unexpected welcome home. It didn't take long, however, before he was pulling her into his arms and returning his own brand of kisses, which she accepted hungrily.

"I may have to slip away again if this is what it's like when a sailor returns home," he chuckled, "but it would've been even nicer to have had you with me all the time."

She placed the meatloaf in the oven with the baked potatoes and then curled up on Cory's lap so he couldn't get away. She had to know where he'd been and what he'd done, but not until she got her fill of kisses and hugs. "It feels so right to be back in your arms, Cory, and I'm not going to let anything make me mistrust you again."

The smells from the kitchen finally brought her out of her contented stupor, and she had to reluctantly get up to toss a salad. He followed her, set the table, and got the drinks, plus a few more kisses before they sat down to eat.

While they ate, she fired questions at him about where he had gone, was he always alone, and how had he been able to dock the boat without any lessons or practice?

He very carefully responded about cruising around Cape Cod Bay, picking up his mother and sister to go with him, and the docking hadn't been that hard because the boat handled so well. He held his breath wondering if he was going to get by without telling her he was an experienced pilot or at least hoping she would accept his explanation like a sweet and beautiful girl in love?

"Cory, is there something about your past that you haven't gotten around to telling me yet? You learned to handle the boat almost too quickly; so did you, by any chance, already know how to pilot a boat before you asked me to teach you? Did my dad know you were an experienced pilot before he willed his pride and joy to you? When I called Donna one day, I asked if you'd had any problems with the boat, and I was sure I heard her chuckle."

"Andrea, Sweetheart, remember you said just a few minutes ago that you weren't going to let anything make you mistrust me again. Did you really mean that?"

Shaking her head and giggling, "You're really too much, Cory Calhoun, but I know now just how lonesome I was while you were gone, not to mention the three weeks before you left. I thought I'd really lost my new friend, so I'll promise not to make a big fuss. Just tell me how experienced you are and how ridiculous you thought I was trying to teach you. Don't try to squirm out of it, though, because I want to know the truth."

"Do you still consider me just a friend after all these kisses—plus your confession of missing me so terribly?" he laughed. "But, to answer your probing question, I didn't think you were ridiculous at all, Sweetheart. You did an excellent job of teaching. I just needed an excuse to be with you, so I could really get to know you, and I thought that was a good way to accomplish it. You would make a good teacher, and I really mean that."

After they had cleaned up the kitchen, he wanted to snuggle up on the new sofa which he'd noticed before but had been too preoccupied to acknowledge. However, Andrea insisted that he see all she had done while they were apart. He got to see all the nice clean closets, her newly painted bedroom, and all the pieces of furniture she'd purchased for the living room. "I gave all the old furniture to a family that my dad had helped several times over the years. I think they have two teenagers, the age that's so hard on couches, and two younger children, so they were especially pleased to get the couch and chairs. She put her arms around his neck and initiated a short, sweet kiss, and he led her to the couch.

He told her about some of the places they had docked, that Fall was a great time to be on a boat because the scenery was beyond description, and that he'd really enjoyed the visit with his mom and sister.

"And now back to us," he said as he covered her mouth with his and couldn't keep his hands from roaming just a little. For Andrea, that sent all sorts of shivers, chills, and tingles up her arms, down her back, and into her stomach as well as bells ringin' in her head, and she quickly pushed away.

"I'm sorry, Cory, but this makes me afraid and I don't know exactly what to do about it. I don't seem to have any will power against you, but I know it would be all wrong to let you continue. I've been going to church again, something I know my dad would appreciate. We haven't really discussed our Christian beliefs, but I'm hoping you'll consider going with me."

"I'd love to attend church with you, Andrea. I haven't been as faithful as I used to be, and I need to re-establish my connection with God. I believe He's there waiting for me to come back to Him, and I want that very much. And, if you're feeling vulnerable, I guess it's up to me to be the strong one tonight. I'm going to get out of here so you can get some real good sleep, and I think I'll sleep real well for a change, too." Getting up from the sofa, he let his eyes travel from her head to her toes, and then said, "Sweet dreams, Sweet One." He pulled her to her feet and with a kiss, a wink, and a whistle, he started toward the door.

"Do you want to sleep here, Cory? How are you going to get home?" she asked as she followed him to the door.

"Sweetie, after being away from you for so long, I wouldn't trust myself to stay here much longer tonight let alone all night. I've been a good boy so far when I've stayed here, and I want to keep my record in tiptop shape with the girl of my dreams. I'm walking home on the good solid ground which, after ten days on the boat, will feel great. I **will** take one more of your delicious kisses, though."

Looking through her binoculars, Grace spotted a boat entering the cove. "A boat's coming, Roger," she remarked as she glanced around to see her husband's reaction. When he wasn't there, she hurried to the porch where she knew she'd most likely find him with his binoculars to his eyes, too.

"Do you think it's Cory?" she asked as she came to stand beside him, and she again positioned her binoculars toward the water.

"Yea, it's Cory, but I wonder what kind of reception he'll receive."

"I hope Andrea has missed him enough to want to give him a chance, especially if she remembers how much it would please her father."

"Well, well, well, will you look at that, Sweetheart? She must've been watching at her window, too. He's tossed her the line, and now she's climbing aboard. I think she may have missed him after all. That's quite a reunion, wouldn't you say?"

"I feel a little guilty spying on them like this, Roger. Maybe we should let them have their privacy while we go and have our own little rendezvous." She gave him a sweet come-hither smile as she fluttered her dark eyelashes, put her hand in his, and pulled him toward the door.

"I love your way of thinking, Mrs. Dayton, and I'm totally at your service." He'd swept her into his arms and headed for their beautiful and most comfortable bedroom.

After the day she had watched Andrea order Cory and Roger out of her house, Grace had decided to stay and keep her eyes on the situation while Roger went to his office in Boston.

He needed to make sure all their projects were progressing on schedule. He'd returned in three days as he couldn't get over the feeling that he was somewhat to blame and wanted to be close at hand, if needed. They had watched as Cory had tried everything to regain her acceptance of their relationship, but nothing had seemed to work. He had gone to her door every night of the first week, but she wouldn't answer his pleas. Later, delivery vans had brought flowers, a huge assortment of nuts and chocolates, and even a Norfolk Pine in a beautiful cache pot, while he spent a lot of time on the boat.

Grace had even visited the bank and reported to Roger that Andrea had looked so very unhappy, but when Cory had come in, she'd immediately gone to the restroom. And then, he'd apparently given up, because a week ago Friday they'd watched as Cory climbed aboard the boat and cruised out of the cove. That afternoon, when Andrea came home from the bank, it wasn't long before they'd seen her running to the dock, checking the cleats, and standing like she was lost as she looked out toward the Bay. They now hope his return will makes things right again for their friend and his search for happiness with the girl he loves.

Now, as they lay in each other's arms, Grace felt so content and just loved the sounds of the water, the wind, and the woods behind their house, not to mention the lack of all the noisy traffic on the street outside their condo in Boston.

"I wish we could stay here permanently," she whispered as Roger now lay on his side admiring her, and then his lips were soon claiming hers.

"Maybe we can, Sweetheart. With the cool two million Mr. Harrington gave us earning interest and the firm doing so well, we just may be able to work something out."

"Oh, Roger, do you really think so?" She sat up and bent her knees so she could put her arms around them, and she had the most captivating smile on her face as she looked over at her handsome husband who was lightly caressing her back.

"What's that look of yours trying to tell me, Grace? Have you already put our condo on the market?"

"Oh, no, Honey, it's just that—uh—you know—well—I'm about three weeks late, and I'm so hoping I've been able to conceive while we've been here."

Roger was speechless for just a moment before he shouted, "I'm going to be a daddy!" He very gently pulled her into his arms and kissed her so tenderly. "I love you with all my heart, Sweetheart," he whispered in her ear. He then looked at her in that devilish way of his, pouted a little bit, and asked, "But how do I know it's mine and not that foolhardy Clayton's? Maybe you like Clayton more than you do me. Did you have an affair with that vagabond?" They were both laughing heartily as he eased her head back onto the pillow, his lips met hers eagerly, and they were in their dream world once again.

When they returned to the porch, they sat huddled together under an afghan as the cool night air was coming in off the water. The house they'd been watching seemed alive tonight with lights, a far cry from what it had been for the past few weeks. They finally saw the door open and Cory came strolling out, but Andrea was also standing there. "Oops," Roger just had to remark, "He must've forgotten something. Ah, yes, another long goodnight kiss. Things are looking up at the Harrington cottage tonight, but I'm surprised he isn't staying over."

"Just remember, Darling, you didn't get to stay over before the wedding either, even though you tried your best to persuade me." She gave him a little poke in his ribs as they both chuckled at the memories.

>>                                                              >>

## Chapter Seven

As Cory strolled along toward his apartment above the law office, he couldn't keep from smiling as he remembered the wonderful welcome he'd received from Andrea when he'd docked earlier this evening. He was also thinking, if she was feeling as vulnerable in his arms as she had said, just how easy it would've been for him to take advantage of her. *But, if I had, how would I have felt afterward. It's much better that I'm headed home and we can both get a good night's sleep.*

He was within a block of his apartment when he felt like someone had slipped out from beside one of the buildings and was following him. He increased his pace and was debating whether or not to make a run for his office door when he heard a shout from the direction of Roger's house. "Cory, behind you." He swung around ready to strike a blow when he was face to face with a young man who appeared as surprised as he was.

"You're Mr. Cal—houn, aren't you, Sir?" he stammered. "I saw you dock your boat earlier today and I was hoping I could maybe talk to you when you came home. I'm in a lot of trouble, Sir, and I need some advice, but I have no one to turn to."

They heard footsteps running toward them, and they both turned to see a figure coming at a pace only guys in excellent physical shape should be trying. The young man started to bolt, but Cory grabbed his arm and convincingly said, "Don't run away, this is a friend of mine. Let's see if there's someway we can help you."

Roger was panting when he reached them and bent over for a few seconds to catch his breath, but then quickly asked, "What is going on? Who are you, anyway?" as he tried to recognize the figure in the darkness.

Cory spoke up, "Let's go in the office and see what is troubling this young man. We'll decide if there is something we can do to help him with his problem. Do you have time to join us, Roger, or is Grace expecting you to come right back?" Chuckling, he remarked, "You had better come in and have a drink of water, at least, before you jog back up that hill. It'll be a little harder going up than it was coming down."

Roger nodded and headed for the office door. Cory still had the arm of the young man in his grip and led him toward the office, also. Once inside, he went to the small office fridge and got sodas for each of them. "Now, let's try to figure out what this is all about. First, we'd better have a name so we don't have to refer to you as the young man any more."

As he looked from Cory to Roger and then back to Cory, the young man had a very profound fear in his eyes, but he finally told them his name was Jason. "Do you have a last name, Jason?" Cory asked.

"You don't need my last name to give me some advice, do you? My dad will kill me if he finds out what I've done, but I guess I couldn't blame him. It's just that he has a quick temper and sometimes reacts before he has the whole story."

"O.K., then, let's hear your story, Jason. We'll both listen calmly and subjectively and then see if we can come up with a solution. We will not show anger or hostility, but will listen as two big brothers who want to help you." Cory glanced at Roger who nodded affirmatively.

With tears welling up in his eyes and trying to wipe them away with the back of his hand, Jason started to speak. "I graduated from High School last spring and wanted to go to college this fall to study Journalism and World History. I want to be a writer, both fiction and non-fiction, and think I could be good at it. I'd written for my High school newsletter, worked on the Yearbook and had gotten a small scholarship to help with the tuition at a Junior College. I found a job for the summer and put every cent I could away. I never thought to put it in the bank because I never dreamed anyone would think there was any money in our house. But one night I came home with my earnings for the week, went to put it away with the rest of my savings, and I found it gone."

He couldn't contain the tears and they rolled down his cheeks. Cory handed him a tissue and waited for him to continue. "I ran to find Mom and Dad but they had gone to the movie and my younger brother and sister were staying with friends. I guess I went rather berserk. I was so angry that I decided if someone did that to me, I could do it to someone, too. I started watching homes and when I knew no one was there, I went in and took things. I had searched for money mostly, but when I couldn't find that, I took some silverware, a couple of pretty silver trays, and a silver pitcher.

I heard my folks talking about the missing items and that the police were looking for the robber, and I realized what I had done. I'd thought there had to be more than one thief, because someone had stolen from me, so maybe they'd nab the other one and consider it a closed case."

"Do you still have the articles you took from the homes, Jason, and just how many homes did you actually enter?"

"I have them hidden in a little shed that's well hidden up on the hill, and I went into three houses, but only took things from two."

Roger looked a little startled, but then started laughing. "You have them hidden in that little shed on my property? Good Lord, the Chief will think I really did turn into a vagabond." He looked at Cory and quickly brought himself back under control.

Cory said, "I wish I'd been here for you, Jason, so you wouldn't have had to go to such extremes, but I think we can work something out. Do you have any idea who might have taken your money? Did you mention it to anyone, like at work or to a friend?"

"I don't think I mentioned it to anyone but my mom and dad. Maybe I said something to my brother since we share the same room. Dad didn't think I needed to go away to college just to be a writer—it was just a waste of time in his books, and he told me there were other things I should be using that money for. He'd worked real hard all his life in construction to provide for mom and us kids, but he was injured two years ago and now is handicapped and in a wheelchair. He has to sit and watch as Mom goes to work each day to clean other people's homes while he does what he can to help around our house. When he was working, he'd gone to some evening classes and learned how to draw blueprints and take off material lists, but he doesn't know anyone who needs his talent now. He has resigned himself to just collecting his disability pay.

I gave them some of my paycheck each week, too, hoping it would make things a little easier and they could find a little happiness together. They are great parents, although as I said, Dad is very strict about doing the right thing, and I know he'd be quite angry about what I've done."

"I think we get the picture, Jason, and we'll let you in on a little story of our own. We were both helped by a great man who became a father figure to us, not that we'd done anything wrong, but nevertheless we benefited greatly from this man's generosity and love of helping others. I'm hoping that some of the wisdom and guidance we received from him will guide us in a way that we can help you. We need to work out a plan to return the items you've taken, and then try to get you enrolled in college for the next semester. Can you stay at your parents' without arousing their suspicions about what you've done?"

"Oh, yes, Sir, but I have no way of entering college for the second semester. I'll just have to continue working and make the best of it, but if you could help me find a way to give back the items without going to jail, I'd be most appreciative."

"Jason, the two of us believe your story, and it warrants a helping hand. We want to see you fulfill your dream, and we're going to do our best to give you a chance to do that.

You go about your regular schedule for the next two days and then meet us here Tuesday night at 8:30. Now, you mentioned looking for money in the houses you went into. Did you find any and, if so, where is it? And, have you been able to put any part of your pay away since your money was stolen?"

"I have the check I got yesterday in my pocket, and I found about $50 in one of the houses. I opened a savings account with that and added last week's paycheck to it. I knew you were gone on the boat so I couldn't talk to anyone until you got back. I was really scared that someone at the bank would ask me about the $50, but they just smiled, when I put my whole paycheck in, so I thought I'd be safe. I was sure hoping you'd be coming back soon."

"Jason, I want you to take your paycheck to the bank tomorrow and add it to your savings account except for the amount you usually give to your parents. Take that home and give it to them and also mention that you're going to put the rest in a safe place. I'm going to give you some money, and I want you to put it exactly where you had been keeping the money before, but don't mention it to your siblings this time. I don't want you to think I'm in any way suspecting your parents, because I'm not. However, just a remark about how proud they are of you for the way you're saving to go to college could be just what sticky fingers want to hear, for example." He pulled his wallet from his pocket and handed Jason two $20's and four $10's.

"Be sure to check to see if it's still there before you come to meet us Tuesday night." He and Roger watched as Jason headed down the street.

"I may have to become Clayton again," Roger said with a grin. "That man can do a lot of snooping around without anyone suspecting a thing."

"You're on the right track, My Friend, but right now we don't have a name or an address or even an employer. Do you have any ideas how we might find some answers?"

"Yep, I do. That boy's story fit some facts I know and he also looked slightly familiar to me. I'm afraid, though, that the one I'll have to talk to will require a real clever interrogation on my part. It'll have to be one that really doesn't look or sound like an interrogation."

"Are you going to let me in on it?"

"Not right at the moment, Cory. Let me do some checking and I'll get back to you about noon tomorrow. How about lunch?"

"Should I bring something in so we'll have the privacy we need?"

"That sounds like a splendid idea, Mr. Attorney."

>>                                                              >>

## Chapter Eight

The next morning Cory went to the bank to do a little investigative business of his own. He headed toward Andrea's desk, and he had to chuckle as he remembered just two or three weeks ago when she would escape to the rest room whenever he'd walked in. Today she had a big smile for him, and his heart was thumping in his chest. *Oh, Andrea, will you some day soon consent to really be mine?*

"It's nice to see you so early in the morning, Cory. Is there something I can do for you or is this just a short and friendly hello?"

"I'd love for it to be a long and friendly hello, Sweetie, but I am actually here on a legal matter. I'm not really sure you can help me, but I was hoping you could refer me to the right person." He had to smile as he noticed the sparkle in those beautiful blue eyes.

"I'll do my best, Mr. Calhoun. This sounds like you came back just in time to really be needed by someone." *I wish I were that person you want me to refer you to. Of course, it'd be nice if it were to love, not just as a friend or to do business with.*

Talking very softly, he said, "I'm hoping I can help a young man with his future as your father helped Roger and me. I'd like to tell you what I know so far, but I need a little more privacy so I don't let something be overheard." She quickly motioned for him to follow her to an office used for confidential transactions, and he gave her a short version of last night's events while she listened intently. "Now, Andrea," he said, "what I need to find out is if there's been a checking account or a savings account opened in the last three weeks for an amount that seems excessive in view of the person's normal financial status."

"Wow, you may be able to solve two cases in one big sweep, and, yes, I can try to help you." Andrea soon had the computer pulling record after record as she scanned the screen. After ten minutes had gone by, Cory was beginning to feel his idea wasn't going to be productive, but then she looked over at him with concern in her eyes. "I have found something, Cory, which looks a little suspicious." She turned back to the screen, clicked a few other entries, and then remarked, "I think I have what you want, but I'll have to check with my supervisor before I can give it to you. Wait here and I'll get right back to you." He noticed that her earlier smile had faded quickly and there was now sadness in her voice.

"What is it, Andrea?" He caught her hand to stop her from leaving because he had a few questions he wanted answered before she brought someone else in. "Do you know the person or family?"

Nodding, she looked at him with tears in her eyes. "I shouldn't say anymore, Cory, but you are an attorney and maybe we can keep it from the supervisor. It's one of the boys in the family I told you that I had given the furniture to. It's the 15 year old, and I think he's a good friend of Samuel who is the brother of one Jason I know. Oh, Cory, I can't even begin to realize what this will do to his parents. Isn't there something we can do to keep this from being broadcast all over town or even worse, the whole country? The way TV picks up stories these days, it could be disastrous for our little community. I'll be more than happy to replace Jason's money and let Craig Norton keep this account."

"That's very sweet of you, Andrea, and we'll definitely help both families, but you know we can't let Craig get by with stealing. Roger is doing some snooping, as he calls it, this morning and we're going to meet for lunch. We'll try to figure out something to save Jason and Craig. By the way, what is Jason's last name? He wouldn't tell us last night. He said we didn't need to know his last name to give him some advice." He couldn't stop a little chuckle and a grin as he remembered the young man who was so afraid he was going to go to prison.

Andrea couldn't help grinning either as she told him the family name was Anderson and that she was sure Jason had an older sister, probably about 22 or 23 now, as well as a brother Sam and a little sister, Janie. In fact, she remembered reading about a wedding a year or so ago.

"What I'd like to have from you right now, Sweetheart, is no supervisor, and if asked, we were talking about your dad's Will and getting your money invested. Will you do that for me? We'll put enough in this bank to satisfy them," he laughed.

She hesitated for just a moment and then nodded. "Just remember, I don't do this for all the handsome young men who come into the bank and make eyes at me."

"I should hope not, but what if this somewhat handsome man were to ask if you'd have dinner with him tonight?" He blinked his eyes to show those long curly eyelashes.

"I'm afraid I couldn't refuse. Are you taking me out or would you like to eat some more of my cooking?"

"I'd love having you to myself, but do you really want to cook?"

"Of course, and I want you to come as soon as you can and plan to stay late because we have a lot of making up to do—over a whole month, to be exact."

"Andrea, My Dear, do you remember that you sent me home last night because you had some problem with my actions? You'd better be careful what you promise to a willing and able young man." Laughing, he blew her a kiss and slipped out the door,

*We'll see,* she thought as she walked back to her desk. *I am over 25 now and maybe I can be a willing and able young woman, too. But maybe not,* she shuddered.

❧

When Roger arrived at noon, Cory sent Donna to lunch with a couple of errands to run for him as well. He felt that would keep her away long enough for the two of them to do some thinking and planning. He was anxious to hear what

Roger had found out and to tell him about what he had learned at the bank.

"Well, were you able to find out anything from the mysterious interrogation?" Cory asked as they got settled in his office and he distributed the lunch he'd had delivered. Roger had an almost devilish smile on his face so he must have some news to share.

"I got enough information to make me think that something is definitely going on in the Anderson home that has Mrs. Anderson rather upset. Our Jason, without a last name, is the son of our housekeeper, and she also has a son named Sam. She opened up to me that Sam has been so quiet lately that it is almost scary, since he's usually the most talkative one in the family. Besides that, he and his friend, Craig Norton, were almost always together, but the kid hasn't been over to their house for over three weeks. She feels they have had a spat of some kind, but he won't talk about it. Looks a little fishy, don't you think?"

"Yes, it certainly does, especially since I was able to track down the money to an account in Craig Norton's name," Cory remarked. "I went to the bank this morning and got Andrea to help me so no one else had to be involved. She knows both families and wanted to help by giving Jason his money back and letting Craig keep his account. I told her that was very sweet of her, but we couldn't let Craig get by with stealing."

"Well, I also stopped to see the Police Chief this morning, and he is quite willing to work with us to see that the stolen articles are returned, if we can produce them," Roger inserted. "He'd also arrange some community service, one task being to put up all the flags and other Christmas decorations on Main Street which would require several boys. He said he'd ask for volunteers at the school and around town so it won't look suspicious that only two or three are doing all the work. There could also be some snow shoveling, spreading sand at store fronts when it's icy, and sweeping it up when the ice is gone.

He apparently is quite fond of Jason and was really surprised that he would resort to such behavior. He could also understand how such an honest, courageous, and outstanding student, as Jason apparently is, would be so devastated when something as important to him as his college education was taken away. So how do you think we should proceed?"

"It's great that we have the Chief on our side. What would you think about this plan? You report to the Chief that Jason has told you the stolen articles are in your shed. The two of you recover the goods, bring them to the station, notify the owners and he can have them come to the station to identify and reclaim. To them, we have no idea how the items got in the shed, and by the way, the $50.00 will need to be among them.

Now, while you're doing that, I'm going to call Mr. and Mrs. Norton and have them come to the office. If they knew about the money, then they're in trouble along with their son, but if not, we'll figure something out that will return the money to Jason, have Craig work with the other volunteers, and help both families improve their financial status."

"Wow, Mr. Attorney, me thinks you've come up with a winner. I'll get right on my part of the deal. It's going to be much easier than you confronting Craig's parents." He stood and started for the door.

"Wait, Roger, I just had another thought. I think Clayton could play a part in this, too. How would he like to stalk Craig for a couple of days, mentioning that he was seen in the bank one day depositing a good amount of money? You can come up with your own dialogue, maybe asking where he got it, what his plans are, and maybe he'd like to share it with you so you don't talk. Do you think it might scare him enough that he might think twice before doing something like this again?"

Roger was grinning from ear to ear. "How absolutely fantastic—you truly are a genius, Mr. Attorney. Grace will be thrilled, too, to have Clayton around again, but I may become a jealous, green-eyed monster. You know, she thinks she may be pregnant, and she's claiming that Clayton may be the father," he laughed as he took his leave.

Shaking his head and smiling at Roger's apparent love for his wife, Cory turned his attention to the task before him, but then it occurred to him that he didn't know for sure if there was a Mr. Norton. Andrea hadn't mentioned anything other than the fact that her dad had helped them several times over the years and that there were four kids. He picked up the phone and had just begun to dial when he heard the outside door open. Had Donna come back or had someone else come in, but almost immediately Andrea appeared at his office door. "May I come in?" she asked.

"Of course, I had just picked up the phone to call you because I need just a little more information that I think you can give me. What brings you by—were you missing me so terribly?"

"Ha Ha. I took a late lunch hour so I could come and find out what you and Roger talked about, what you found out besides the bank account and what you've decided to do. I saw that his car wasn't around so I assume you finished your discussion."

Grinning, he motioned for her to come over to him. "I couldn't get a good morning kiss at the bank earlier, but I can now. Donna isn't back yet and I have you all to myself in a cozy office just built for two." She hadn't moved so he stood up and walked over to shut the door behind her. His arms went around her waist from the back and he drew her back so she was up against him. He lifted her hair so he could kiss the nape of her neck, then around to nibble on her earlobe as he was turning her around to face him. Just as he was tilting her chin so he could put his lips on hers, he thought he heard a soft knock and the doorknob turning.

Donna peeked in and said, "I'm back—Oh, I'm sorry, I didn't know you were that busy." Laughing, she closed the door again and Cory returned to his uncompleted kiss.

"What did you say you dropped by for, Miss Harrington?" he asked as they were just finishing their third or fourth kiss.

"Just this, I guess, because I've got to get back to the bank now. I'll have to wait until later to find out about you and Roger. Does Donna know what you two are doing?"

Cory shook his head. "No, I thought it better to talk to Roger first and come up with some ideas before confiding in anyone else. I know Donna can keep it confidential because that is part of her job and she has done it for years. She came with me from Boston so she knows the rules of an attorney's office very well."

"That's another story I want to hear about, but it will have to wait, too. I'll see you as soon as you can get away. I'll be home by 4:00 and I'm cooking. Bye, now!"

"Oh, Andrea," he called as she was hurrying through the outer office. She returned, but her blushing face told him she was embarrassed having to face Donna. "I'm sorry to call you back," he said grinning, "but I'd like to know what Mr. Norton does for a living, or is there a Mr. Norton?"

"You can wipe that grin off your face, Mr.Calhoun, and yes, there's a Mr. Norton. He works as a yardman at the lumberyard and Do-it-yourself Center just outside of town. He makes a fairly good salary, but with four kids, it doesn't go very far these days."

"You're so right. Thanks, Sweetie, I'll see you later," he said with the big grin still on his face. After finding the Norton number in the phone book, Cory saw no reason to put off calling, and Mrs. Norton answered on the third ring. Cory explained that he would like to talk to her and her husband concerning a case he's working on. He needed to determine if they could possibly be witnesses since their names had come to his attention. She was a bit hesitant, asking what the case was about and when had it occurred, but Cory told her he'd rather tell them face to face. It was decided that they would come tomorrow afternoon at 2 o'clock since Mr. Norton has Tuesday afternoons off. Cory was elated because he felt they might have all the details in place by the time Jason came back to see them that evening.

Roger had gone back to the Police Station, explained to the Chief what he and Cory had planned, and they immediately left to retrieve the stolen items. The Chief would handle the return of the pieces to the rightful owners so Roger and Cory would not be involved in that at all.

Roger then headed home to tease Grace a little, When he walked through the door, he called, "Hey, Sweetheart, I have some great news for you, Clayton is coming back so you'll get to see your heart—throb—again," he trailed off. "Honey, what is wrong?" he asked as he fell on his knees beside her chair. She had her head on the table and her hands holding her stomach,

Raising her head and with the biggest smile, she said, "I've been so sick to my stomach today, Roger. Isn't it wonderful?"

"It's wonderful that you're sick?" he looked at her with a puzzled look on his face. "Should I call the doctor?"

"The baby, Silly, I'm starting some morning sickness, but I think I may be one who's going to be sick longer than just mornings—to start with anyway. I do need to go to Boston to see my gynecologist, though, so what's this about Clayton coming back? Not for long, I hope."

"Forget about Clayton, Grace. Do you want to leave this afternoon? You know your needs always come first."

"No, I'll call and make an appointment after you tell me what Clayton has to do. It could be several days before she can see me. You know how busy she is."

Watching her with so much concern in his eyes, he told her about the plans Cory had come up with, his day so far, and what he planned to do to convince Craig that he had done something wrong and people knew about it.

"Clayton can do that, I'm sure," she giggled as she leaned over to give him a sweet kiss and to tell him he could get up off his knees.

❧

Cory had almost forgotten he had an appointment at 2:30 with a paying client, but he found himself more anxious to concentrate on Jason, Sam, and Craig than the transfer of a deed.

*What is Samuel's role in all this?* Cory wondered after the appointment was over. *Is he the reason Craig knew about the money being in the house? Does that explain Samuel being so quiet like Mrs. Anderson had mentioned to Roger? There are still some loose ends, I fear.*

A knock on his office door made Cory jump because he'd been in such deep thought. "Come in," he called and Clayton peeked his head in. "Donna wasn't at her desk. I'm on my way to find Craig now, but thought I'd check in. The Chief has the items and will see that they're returned. Did you have any luck with the Nortons?"

"I'm meeting with them tomorrow afternoon. Mr. Norton has Tuesday afternoons off so they're coming in to see if I can use them for witnesses in one of my cases."

"Oh, that's good, Cory. By the way, I've got to tell you—Grace has started having morning sickness so we'll be making a trip to Boston as soon as I finish with Craig. I hope a few days away won't hurt, but I have to take care of my baby."

"You'd better believe you do. I'm so excited for you and probably a little envious, too, because I'd love to be in your shoes. But, before you get away, what do you think about Sam? Do you think he's involved at all?"

"I don't think we need to worry about Sam right now. Mrs. Anderson said she was trying to find out why he's being so quiet. I think when we get Craig to confess, Sam will come around with any information he has."

"Maybe Jason will get to him by tomorrow night, too. Do you want to be in on that or do you want to get on your way to Boston?"

"I told Grace I needed to be here for a couple of days so she's going to call for an appointment and see when her gynecologist can see her. It may not be until next week so we should be fine to complete this case."

"O.K. then, if not before, I'll see you tomorrow night around 8:00 or 8:30."

"I'll be here, but now Clayton is off to have some fun."

*And Cory is, too,* he mused. *My sweet little innocent Andrea is in for a big surprise tonight after her remark this morning about us making up for a lot of lost time.* Chuckling, he knew he wouldn't take advantage of her, but he thinks she deserves a little payback for what she was hinting, or at least how a man would most likely take it.

He closed his office door, asked Donna if she would see that the front door was locked, and he was on his way to a rendezvous with a very naive young lady, but, oh how he loves that little sweetheart. She has his heart hopping, skipping, and jumping, but he still can't figure out exactly how she feels about him. A little remark here and there has his hopes rising, and then it seems she can push him away as if they're really only friends. *Oh, well, I have time to gain some winning points while she decides if she can really love the one her father picked for her.*

He has a few minutes to do some errands as he begins his walk toward the cottage, but he is so anxious to see what Andrea was really thinking when she made that statement at the bank this morning. Will she take the initiative to take their relationship just a little bit farther? He really doubts it, but it'll be fun trying to find out what she had in mind.

>>                                                                    >>

*Chapter Nine*

Cory made two important stops on the way to the cottage. *I've got to make a good impression if I'm going to win her heart,* he kept reminding himself. He knocked, like a gentleman should, and waited for her to come and invite him in, but he had his face hidden behind a dozen long-stemmed roses when she opened the door. "Surprise," he said as he peeked around the bouquet and grinned at her.

"Oh, Cory, they're beautiful, and you're so sweet to bring them. Please, come in." She took the roses he'd handed to her and headed for the kitchen.

*Whoa, that isn't the way it's supposed to go,* so he quickly followed and caught her at the kitchen sink. Taking the flowers from her hands, he placed them on the counter and then slowly turned her around to face him and backed her up against the counter, pinning her there with his arms. He moved closer so his body was up against her and his mouth claimed hers in a very passionate kiss. His hands left the counter and his arms encircled her waist, but they were soon inching up her back until he thought they were in a great position to tilt her back with one hand and his other could move around to cup her breast. He hoped his kisses would keep her in his spell, but he could hear the gulp in her throat and also feel her hands quickly move to his chest to push him away. He tried to hold her tighter against him and continue to kiss her as he uttered an Uh Uh.

She jerked her head quickly so the kiss was broken and then gave him a slight push. "Uh Uh is right, Cory," she gasped. "You're not supposed to do that."

"Uh huh," he replied as his lips caressed her cheek, the tender spot below her ear, and then back to her lips.

Again she broke the kiss and pushed him away. "Cory, I thought we were just to be friends. That's what you said the day we met and read Dad's Will."

As he dropped his hands and backed away, he said, "I thought at the time that if I said anything other than that it would scare you off, but do you want to be just friends after all the kisses we've shared the last few weeks, not to mention the morning I saw you in that thin nightgown?" He just had to flutter those long dazzling eyelashes and flash that devilish grin. "Remember, Sweetie, you're the one who told me this morning that we had a whole lot of catching up to do. Just what did you mean by that, anyway?"

He had to chuckle as her face was blushing red and she stammered, "I—I'm really not sure. I-I think my th-thoughts and de-desires got a-ahead of my good sense. Please, Cory, don't push me too fast, okay? I've always dreamed of still being a virgin when I got married, but I'm afraid you could convince me to destroy that dream." Tears were now welling up in her eyes and Cory immediately took her back in his arms.

"Sweetheart, you're in no danger of me going too far and ruining that dream for you, because I want you to remain the virgin you want to be until you write your name on a marriage certificate, whoever the lucky guy is." *I sure hope it'll be me.* "I was just teasing you a little because of your unexpected statement this morning. I must say, though, a little touching never hurt anybody, and I think you might enjoy it," he grinned as his hand started back toward her, but she slapped it away and turned back to the roses.

"Why don't you go watch TV? I'll put the casserole in the oven and set the table. The salad is already made so I'll join you shortly."

"I'd rather stay and watch you while I let my imagination form some very exciting pictures of what is under those pretty clothes you're wearing."

"Cory!" she shouted, "stop that kind of talk. You don't sound anything like that guy I met at the attorney's office."

"Okay, but I am a guy," he chuckled. "I'll tell you about my afternoon instead. Mr. and Mrs. Norton are coming in tomorrow afternoon, and Clayton is tracking down Craig before he and Grace go to Boston for a few days. She has had some morning sickness so wants to see her gynecologist. Tomorrow night we meet with Jason, and possibly a few others, depending on what happens tonight and tomorrow afternoon."

"I'm so happy for Grace and Roger. I'm looking forward to having morning sickness some day."

"Would you really like to be in that condition, Andrea?"

"Definitely, after I find a husband who I'm sure loves me as much as it appears that Roger loves Grace."

"What would it take to convince you that a guy does love you that much?"

"I'll just know, Cory, so don't try to make something specific be your magic touch." Her immediate blush told him she had realized she'd used the word 'touch' and now felt a bit embarrassed. She hurriedly slipped the casserole in the oven, picked up the tray of snacks she'd been fixing, and said, "Let's go in the living room and put some food in our mouths so maybe I can keep my foot out of mine."

He was laughing as he got a couple of soft drinks from the fridge and followed her, admiring the long satiny blonde hair, the sexy swing of her small hips, and those nice slender legs.

"We need to have Roger and Grace over, when they return from Boston, so we can get to know each other—without Clayton, of course," Andrea started the conversation as they got settled on the couch. "Maybe we could have a Thanksgiving dinner, Cory. I'm sure that Roger doesn't have any close family, but I don't know about Grace. Maybe your mom and sister could come, too."

"You would want to do that? It's an awful lot of work to fix a Thanksgiving dinner, especially when you're working." He noticed a grin spreading across her face and he got the message loud and clear. "You're thinking about quitting your job, aren't you, Andrea? When did you make that decision? I think it's wonderful—we can get away whenever we want, we can make some concrete plans,—but I'm just assuming," he finished in a whisper, "that you'd want me to be a part of your life, aren't I? But, Sweetheart, would that really be so bad? You do remember, don't you, that's what your dad wants?"

"My dad wanting something, Cory, doesn't make it right. I told you earlier that I do want a husband who loves me like Roger loves Grace, without reservations or hesitation. I can't live my life just to please my father. He's gone and I'm here, all by myself, with only a wonderful new friend who would sacrifice his own happiness to please a dead man. You can't imagine how sad that makes me feel. I love your company, Cory, and I know how much I missed you when you were gone, but I can't expect you to devote your life to me just because my father asked you to."

"Oh, Andrea, you haven't listened to a word I've said for the last six weeks if you think I've been spending time with you because of your father's request. When I opened my office door and saw you for the first time, before we even opened your father's Will, my heart was pounding, my palms were sweaty, and I wasn't sure I could even talk, but I would've almost been willing to marry you right then, I was so captivated.

And I still am—so much so that I want you to wear an engagement ring until we can be married and live here as man and wife, and you can have morning sickness as often as you want. We'll enlarge the house to accommodate them all," he grinned. He pulled a small box from his pocket, slipped onto his knees, and opened it so she could see the beautiful solitaire diamond mounted on a lovely, delicate gold band. "I love you, Andrea Harrington, and when I couldn't make you listen to me for three weeks, I couldn't do anything but leave here and try to overcome my disappointment. You'll never know my elation when you came to the dock and welcomed me home so lavishly. I'll cherish you for as long as I live, and if you want to get married tomorrow, we can fly to Las Vegas and say our vows. Will you make me the happiest man in the world tonight by saying you'll marry me?"

"Oh, Cory, are you sure you want to marry me? I've been such a thorn in your side with all my idiotic ideas, my throwing you and Roger out of the house and refusing to even talk to you. Are you sure this isn't because my dad coerced you into doing it? I'm sorry, but you must admit, some things that have happened aren't too easy to believe."

"One thing I hope you will believe, because it's very, very true, is that I have loved you from the first night we were together and went for that boat ride. I haven't wanted you out of my sight from that moment on. Can you imagine my despair when I thought Clayton might harm you? But, Honey, will you let me put this ring on your finger so I can get up off the floor. I think my leg is going to sleep."

She smiled, giggled, and even laughed nervously as she held out her hand for him to slip the ring on her finger so slowly and tenderly while he whispered all kinds of sweet nothings to her. They had a marvelous kiss to seal the engagement, but then he said, "I don't ever want to let go of your hand, Sweetheart, but could I be smelling an overdone casserole?"

"Oh, no." Running to the kitchen, she pulled the casserole from the oven. It was just a little crusty around the edges, but the center was still good. With the salad she'd made, and some hot rolls, they enjoyed their meal together, ending with cake and ice cream.

When they'd finished putting the dishes in the dishwasher, they went back to the couch and as she sat at the edge of the cushion trying to stretch out some of the stress of the day, he started massaging her back. He pulled her back toward him and by starting at her shoulders, he felt the tight muscles as he rubbed them tenderly. He knew she wasn't in a very comfortable position so he suggested she lie on her bed so he could do a better job.

Immediately she was on the defensive. "Now I understand how you operate, Cory Calhoun. You'll go so far as to buy a beautiful ring just to get a woman into a bed. Well, it's not going to happen—you can just get out of here and take your ring with you!" As she tried to get the ring off her finger, Cory scooped her up in his arms and headed for her bedroom. She was kicking and screaming at him, but he wouldn't release her until he got her to the bed and dropped her in the middle of it, face down. He straddled her quickly so she couldn't move and proceeded to massage her back muscles until she could do nothing but relax.

A few minutes later, she was asleep and he sat on the edge of the bed smiling at the wild tigress he was going to marry. "I'm going to love every minute of my life with you, Andrea Harrington," he whispered as he quietly went around the house checking the doors, turning off lights, and then, after taking off his shoes and socks, he crawled onto the bed beside her. He was wondering what she'd do when she awoke and found him on her bed. It should be quite a ruckus. With a smile on his face, he fell asleep.

❦

Cory was the first to wake, and it was just beginning to lighten for a new day. He was certainly surprised to find that he had a blanket over him, and when he glanced over to see Andrea, she was under the covers on her side of the bed. *Well, she didn't kick me off onto the floor, anyway, but how did she do all that without waking me? I guess I'm not a very good protector if I sleep through being covered with a blanket and letting her get in and out of bed.* He carefully turned on his side so he could watch her as she slept, and he realized she'd even been able to take off the clothes she'd been wearing because her arm, which was out of the covers, was in a nightgown. *I wonder if it's another old thin one.*

He thought he heard his name being spoken very softly so he listened closely. She faced away from him but he still heard her sleepy, sweet little voice say, "Cory, I do love you, but will you love me like Roger loves Grace?"

He knew then that he had to find a way to convince her that he truly did love her and he'd been captivated from the first day he'd met her. It was a little strange because he'd heard so much about her from Mr. Harrington that he'd been determined not to like her. He thought no one could be as perfect as her dad had described, so she would naturally be a spoiled brat. Actually, her dad had tried at least two or three times to have them meet, but he'd always been able to come up with a good excuse.

*That was probably why Mr. Harrington had to resort to the codicil to his Will. Oh, how wrong and selfish I've been. If*

*I'd agreed to meet her, her dad might have had the pleasure of walking her down the aisle. Of course, there's always the chance that she wouldn't have been ready to accept my proposal then since it wasn't the easiest thing I've done to get the ring on her finger now. I'll have to try and find a way to make it up to her.*

She started to stir and for a moment he didn't know what he should do—get out of her room as quickly as possible, or take her in his arms and snuggle. Suddenly it was too late to leave as she rolled over on her back, looked at him and smiled. She then turned on her side to face him. "Good morning, Cory, did you know you're a very sound sleeper? Someone could've carried you away last night and you would've slept right through it." She brought her hand up to his face and caressed his bristled cheek as she moved even closer and planted a good morning kiss on his lips. "Thank you for the massage," she whispered. "I haven't slept so well in ages."

"I could do that for you every night, if you'd like," he murmured as his hand stroked her shoulder and neck and then ran his fingers through her hair that lay so soft and inviting on her pillow. His lips were starting toward hers, but the tightness he was feeling in his clothes made him realize he was still wearing his dress pants and shirt. "When did you wake up and change into your gown and put this blanket over me?" he asked as he caressed her cheek with the back of his hand. "I'll have to get a watch dog to keep track of you."

She giggled. "It was about midnight, I think. I was a little chilly, which is probably the reason I woke up, so I decided to change into my gown and crawl under the covers. It was dark and I didn't realize you were there at first, but then I tried to wake you so you could go into Dad's room. You wouldn't budge so I put the blanket over you. I would've gone to the other room, but I knew my bed would be so nice and warm under where I'd been lying, and I didn't want to get into another cold one."

"So, Miss Harrington, you knowingly let me sleep beside you the rest of the night? My, my, what are the gossips going to do with that bit of news?" Chuckling, he slipped his arm under her neck, his mouth found her lips, and when she responded to his urging her lips to part, he deepened the kiss. "Maybe we could just stay here all day, Sweetie. I could do some of my fabulous massaging and who knows what other marvelous things we might think of doing."

"That's not possible, Mr. Calhoun, because you have a law office calling, and I have a bank to help run. Duty calls." She patted his cheek and started to roll toward her side of the bed when his arm went under the covers, around her waist, and pulled her back toward him.

"Darn these clothes," he protested as he tried to maneuver his body so he could kiss her in a different position. Her little giggle made him so frustrated he was ready to strip his clothes off, but then he realized she had turned and was facing him again. What a reward as her kiss was so soft and sweet. "Do you have time for some more smooching?" he asked as his lips were brushing across hers. He didn't wait for an answer as he continued to kiss her cheek and forehead, nibbled her earlobe and then back to her lips. His mouth then moved to her neck and started a slow series of kisses down toward the low cut bodice of her gown.

Andrea couldn't stop her body from arching, which scared her, and then her gown slipped from her one shoulder. Cory's hand went lightly across the thin gown, as his lips continued their downward trek to the rounded top of the breast that had just been partially exposed by the slipping of the gown. He carefully pulled the gown back up over her bare shoulder, and she uttered a moan that surprised both of them, but then the sensational feelings caused her to gasp, "Cory," but that was all she could say.

"I'm sorry, Andrea, I guess I got carried away," he whispered as he lowered his face and kissed each breast through the cloth of the gown. He grinned when he saw the look on her face as his lips came to rest on hers again. "Did you enjoy that, Sweetheart?" he asked when he'd completed the kiss.

Andrea was so shocked, or aroused, she couldn't move and just lay there staring at him. When she finally could speak, her face was truly blushed when she asked, "Was that part of showing real love, Cory, or was it what they call lust or physical attraction with true feelings not needed? I dated some in college and during the year I lived in New York, but a kiss at the door was all I'd ever allow. No wonder I had so few calls for second dates," she giggled, "and then I came here to be with Dad. I didn't realize I'd missed so much."

"Wow, Andrea, I don't know what to say. I'm really surprised that you've dated so little and are innocent of all the wonderful acts of love. But, on the other hand, I'm thrilled to be the one to show you all that I know, which isn't a whole lot, but maybe we can invent a few great new things of our own," he grinned. He reached for her left hand to make sure the ring was still on her finger, gave it a kiss and then slipped off of the bed. He couldn't believe that he was still on top of the covers and she was still beneath them. *Not for too long, I hope, for then we'll be man and wife.*

"Cory, my dad's clothes are still in his closet if you want to see if anything will fit you. I think he was about your size, wasn't he?"

"Yes, I believe he was and I'll accept your offer because these clothes aren't very presentable to be seen in after our very interesting night." Chuckling, he headed for her dad's bedroom, a nice shower, and hopefully some clothes he could at least wear to his apartment.

Andrea continued lying on the bed, stretching and smiling and looking at the ring on her left ring finger. She glanced at the clock on the nightstand and moaned. *Yep, I think I'll turn in my resignation today. If this is what marriage consists of, I want a lot more of it without having to get up and go to work.* She heard the shower going in her dad's bedroom, so she pulled her robe on and headed for the kitchen. She was hungry and wanted to fix a nice breakfast for Cory. The coffee was brewing quickly and she got the skillet out for bacon and eggs. It occurred to her that she had a package of blueberry muffin mix in the pantry so she stirred up a batch of the large size muffins. Her dad had liked them so well at the cafe that they'd bought the new baking tin on a trip to Boston so she could also make them at home. These might not be as good as her homemade ones, but they'll have to do today.

Everything was ready when Cory came into the kitchen sniffing at the smell of all the good things to eat. "Do you want to fill your own plate, Cory, so you get the amount you want, or would you rather be waited on?" she smiled.

"I'd better fix it myself and not take too much or I may have trouble with your dad's pants. Man, he must have really exercised to stay in shape because his waist was just a bit smaller than mine. I think I'll get busy on my treadmill and try to get a few pounds taken off because, if you don't mind, I'd love to wear some of your dad's clothes. They are really nice and I haven't taken time to buy many clothes since I moved down here."

"That would be wonderful and I know Dad would love it that someone he knew and loved could get some wear out of them. A few things probably should go to the dry cleaners, but we'll go through them and get that done soon. Would you mind if I went and took my shower now? I'll probably be late for work, but that's all right. Maybe they'll fire me." She was giggling as she left the room.

*I love that girl,* he almost shouted as the food disappeared from his plate. *From her giggles to her kisses, from her cooking to her pure innocence, from her spirit of fun to her determination to be taken seriously, she is my idea of an ideal partner for life.* He took his empty plate to the sink, rinsed it off and put it in the dishwasher. He glanced at his watch and realized he'd better be on his way.

He peeked into her bedroom to say goodbye and caught her sitting at the dressing table brushing her hair. She was still in bra and panties with a short robe around her, and he could hardly keep himself from demanding a few more kisses. He bravely, however, just walked over and gave her a quick kiss and whispered, "I'll see you later, maybe in the same outfit?" He was chuckling as he'd almost reached the front door and decided to tease her a little. "You'd better come and lock the door, Sweetheart. You wouldn't want Clayton to come walking in and find you in such a 'come take me' outfit."

She came running out of the bedroom, trying to get her robe tied around her waist, but he didn't see the brush in her hand until it was in the air and aimed for his head. He'd ducked just in time, but it sailed past him and hit the glass window in the front door which, of course, shattered into a thousand pieces. "Now see what you've done, Cory Calhoun? You made me break a window with a brush intended for you," but she was sobbing as she ran into his arms.

"I could've broken your head instead of the window. Oh, Cory, will I ever learn to think before I act?"

"You really are my wild tigress, aren't you? The day you tossed Roger and me out of the house, he remarked that you hadn't changed a bit since you were a part of the small group of kids around town, and he wished me luck trying to tame you. But, Sweetie, I don't want to change you because I love you just the way you are. You make my life very, very interesting, even a bit dangerous at times, but I'm an attorney and you may help me solve a case one day with your wildness. I'll call the Home Center and have someone come to fix the glass. Do get dressed and go to work. They'll probably get the job done a lot easier and faster if you're not here."

He grabbed her fist as it came toward him, pulled her back into his arms and kissed her until she went limp. He then scooped her up and dropped her on the bed before he once again headed for the door, but she was right behind him. "Just going to lock the door," she said sweetly as she poked her hand through the broken window to wave goodbye.

>>                                                                                      >>

# Chapter Ten

Cory hadn't been in the office long before he heard a familiar voice talking to Donna and then footsteps on to the door of his office. "Good morning, Roger, what brings you around so early this morning? Clayton found Craig and you have a good report, I hope?"

Shutting the door behind him, Roger strolled over to one of the leather chairs and looked at Cory with a very wicked smile on his face. "We'll get to Craig in a few minutes, but I was wondering if I can get any information on your overnight stay at Andrea's. I'm sorry that it's a direct view from our house to the cottage, but it was Mr. Harrington's pick of houses, you know. You certainly had a rather destructive exit this morning so we were curious if the whole night followed that pattern? Grace is dying to know just what caused the window in the front door to be broken."

"Yea, I can imagine that it's Grace who is so nosey, but to satisfy your curiosity—it was an up and down sort of evening. It started with a casserole that got a little over-done in spots due to a very serious conversation we were having concerning our future. We ate it, it was very good, and then we cleaned the kitchen. She was rubbing her neck and stretching her back, so I got started on a massage because I could see that she was tired. After a few minutes, I suggested that we finish the massage on her bed where I thought she would be more comfortable.

Of course, she didn't take it that way and almost threw me out again, but I aptly prevailed and she fell asleep, leaving me to sleep beside her on top of the covers, fully dressed. I woke this morning to find a blanket over me while she was under the covers in her nightgown while I was still fully dressed. While I was in the shower, she fixed us a fine breakfast with good blueberry muffins to top it off, but when I was leaving, I mistakenly mentioned that she'd better lock the door so Clayton couldn't walk in on her when she wasn't completely dressed. That led to her throwing her hairbrush at me, but I ducked and it hit the window. Does that give you a clear enough picture of a night with my wild tigress? It was the most exciting night I've spent in my life."

Roger was laughing so hard he started hiccupping and shaking his head. "You do like wild little things, don't you? It actually does sound rather exciting, but when I think about it, Grace gave and gives me some exciting times, too. Oh well, so much for a night of wonder, although not too fulfilling."

"Whoa, who said it wasn't fulfilling? We're both on the same wave length, Roger, when it comes to marriage first, fulfillment later. If I had really pushed, I probably could've made it a love-filled night, but I want her to have the kind of wedding night she has always dreamed about, and I don't plan to do anything to spoil that."

"Sorry, Cory, I guess after four great years of, what do they call it, marital bliss, I have a hard time remembering what it was like before that great day. Grace didn't break any windows or kick me out of the house, but she wouldn't let me stay overnight, either. I think we're two lucky guys and I do wish you the best with Andrea. She was always a sweet one."

"That reminds me—Andrea says she would like to have a Thanksgiving dinner if the two of you are going to be here over the holiday. We knew you didn't have any close family, but we weren't sure about Grace. We've thought about inviting my mother and sister, too."

"That sounds great, Cory, and Grace will be thrilled. She has mentioned wanting to get together with the two of you, and I'm sure she'll want to help. After all, Andrea is still working so it'll be a lot of work for her. You know, if you need beds, we have a few extra bedrooms. And, about Grace's family—she'd been estranged from them since she wouldn't go to the college of their choice. She worked her way through two years at a Junior College and then, as you might expect, she met Mr. Harrington and he paid her tuition for the two final years at BC to major in Finance. Can you imagine the pleasure he must've enjoyed while helping so many in his lifetime?"

"He was one great guy, that's for sure, but as much as I'd like to continue this very interesting conversation, Roger, I have a client coming in this morning so I need to get prepared. Do you have any information on Craig to tell me before I have to kick you out of my office?" he laughed.

"I did see him and I laid it on pretty thick that I had seen him through the window of the bank on the day he deposited a good handful of bills. I hinted that maybe he should share some with me, to help keep my mouth shut, because I was sure I knew where he had gotten all that money. I could tell he was really scared, but he put up a pretty good front.

I thought Clayton would wander around again this afternoon and see what he can find out, but I'll get out of here now so you can meet with your client and make some real money. Let's see, you meet with Craig's parents this afternoon, don't you? Anything you want me to help you with there?"

"No, I'll be fine with them. Are you going to be here at 8:30 to meet with Jason?"

"Yep, I'm planning to be here tonight and then Grace and I will leave for Boston in the morning to get her checked out. I'll meet with my office staff, and then we'll return over the weekend, most likely, unless the doctor wants more tests done. So, good luck this afternoon, and I'm out of here."

"Thanks, and if I don't get a chance tonight to tell you, we'll be praying for an 'All's Well' from the gynecologist. With your binoculars trained on us, you must know that we've been attending church every Sunday. Maybe you'll join us when you return. It really makes quite a difference in the way you look at life. See you tonight."

About fifteen minutes later, the first appointment was announced by Donna. A young man came in that Cory would guess was not much over 20 years old, and Cory could see the tears welling up in his eyes. He knew this was a divorce case, but he didn't expect it to be so emotional for the guy.

Cory tried to be understanding and helpful as he found out the reason for this action. His name was Bryan Munson, and he and Marilee had eloped when they were 20. They had both just finished their sophomore year in college. Now, two years later, she'd realized there were responsibilities attached to a marriage and that it isn't all fun and games. She just wants to return to her parents, go back to school, and get him out of her life.

After listening to Bryan's side of the story, Cory asked if he thought the two of them would be willing to get counseling, but when that didn't sound feasible, he asked if Bryan would be willing to talk to him and Andrea alone some day soon?"

"Andrea Harrington?" he asked. "I knew her before she left for college because she was in the small group of kids that hung around together here. We were all different ages, but I think we were all friends. I liked Andrea and she always treated me real nice although I was about three years younger. Yea, I'd be willing to talk to the two of you anytime since I had to take the first semester off because of the divorce. It's my senior year, and you can imagine that my parents aren't too happy with me about any of this. Are you and Andrea married or planning to be?"

"No definite plans as yet," he offered, and then said, "O.K., Bryan, let me talk to her and see what her schedule is and then we'll get back to you. It shouldn't be long because we need to get some things worked out before Marilee takes you to court. Don't worry, we'll try our best to save the marriage if that is what you want."

"Oh, yes, Sir. I love her very much and want our marriage to last for a long time."

The second appointment was a simple question he could answer about setting up a trust for a daughter who is handicapped. The actual execution of the trust would be at a later date.

It was now lunch time and just as he was considering going to the bank to see if Andrea could join him, her sweet little face peeked in the door. "Are you still speaking to me?" she asked as she walked in and plopped down in the closest chair. "I've had a busy morning, I'm hungry, and I'd like to have some company. Do you have time to join me?"

"You bet. I was just getting ready to go to the bank and ask you to join me when you walked in. Are you ready to go?"

"Let's go to the cottage and see if the window has been fixed, and then I'll fix some lunch for us there." She couldn't read the strange look on his face so she asked, "Isn't that all right?"

*Does she know what she's letting herself in for? No, I'm going to be a very good person because I have a rather difficult meeting this afternoon. I'll just get a few kisses. No, Cory, not even a few kisses because that could lead to forgetting all about this meeting with Mr. and Mrs. Norton. Just eat lunch, just eat lunch, just eat lunch.*

"I think we'd better get something at the cafe, Sweetheart, because I have a very important meeting at 2:00, and I have some things to get straight in my head before they arrive. The window inspection can wait until you get off work, can't it? They did promise to get it installed today."

"All right, Cory, let's go to the cafe. If you're afraid I'll throw something else at you, we'd better stay away from the cottage." She was grinning as she took his hand, grabbed his jacket, and pulled him along through the outer office. Donna was away from her desk, so Cory took time to lock the door and then joined her on the sidewalk.

They walked hand in hand to the cafe, and when they were seated with their soup and a sandwich, Andrea surprised him with the conversation she started. "I've been giving some thought to how we could enlarge the cottage, Cory, and I want to get started with the work as soon as the weather is suitable in the Spring. In your spare time, would you give some thought to it, too, and then we'll have fun comparing notes. We may have to hire an architect for finalizing, but I want our own ideas, not an outsider's, to show in the final plans."

Cory was taken aback as she had never mentioned enlarging the cottage before, and she hadn't even made a comment on his remark the other night about building enough rooms for all the morning sicknesses she wanted to go through. *Is she really serious about getting married and starting a family, or is she just a very organized person who wants things to be done and ready for occupancy before she takes the big plunge. She's apparently very, very much like her father.* "I'd be happy to do that, Andrea, but what got you thinking about this adding on to the cottage all of a sudden. You've never mentioned it before."

She gave him that captivating smile that always sends his hormones off the scale, and in that sweet demure voice said, "You did, Cory, when you mentioned making room enough for all my morning sicknesses. I realized that more than one child would cramp our space in the cottage, and I'm definitely planning on more than one child. We have to start a family tree that will have many branches over the years. I don't want to hear any of our children or grandchildren saying I'm an only child so I don't have any siblings or cousins. You do surely realize, don't you, that ours will only have one aunt to share? We need to do something about a few cousins before it's too late."

"Andrea, what are you saying? Don't tell me you're planning to fix my sister up with a husband before you've even met her. Oh, what a splendid idea!" he laughed. "Do you have anyone in mind?"

"Well, no, but there has to be someone who would be attracted to those long dark eyelashes, but I need some more information about her. Has she dated much, does she have a boyfriend, does she have favorite things she likes to do, why is she still living at home with your mother, how tall is she and what color are her hair and eyes?—you know, statistics."

"Oh, those things. I'm a man, Sweetheart. I don't notice those things about my sister. Those observations are reserved for more interesting subjects," he chuckled.

"Mr. Calhoun, I believe you're making fun of me when I'm trying so hard to simply improve the future of our children, grandchildren, great-grandchildren, and so on. Please get serious and in the next few days, I want some answers on both of these projects."

The server was standing beside their table smiling as she waited to ask them if they wanted a dessert or another drink. Glancing around, they realized that the cafe had almost cleared out from the noon rush, and it was after 1 o'clock. "No, thank you, Doris, we've got to get back to work before our careers go down the drain or up in flames." Handing her two or more bills, he told her to keep the change for letting them have the table so long.

"It sounded as if you were discussing a very serious problem about the future of your family. I hope you'll cooperate with her, Mr. Calhoun, because I think Andrea has a very legitimate concern there. Children really do need siblings, aunts, uncles, and some cousins to make their lives complete."

"Yes, Doris, I do listen to almost everything this young lady has to say, and I'm sorry you didn't get to hear the whole conversation." Chuckling, he put his arm across her stiffened shoulders and then whispered in her ear. "I appreciate your concern, Doris, but will you try to remember that some conversations are supposed to be private?"

"That's right, Mr. Calhoun, but I was just standing up for my female friends. You attorneys always seem to see things so differently than anyone else. It's like you're in a whole other world, but we like you anyway," she smiled. "Have a nice afternoon now, both of you."

Cory took Andrea's hand and led her toward the door, still chuckling. "What would we guys do without all you women trying to run our lives?"

"It would be a terribly boring and unproductive life, Mr. Calhoun. You've heard the saying 'Behind every great man, there's a woman,' haven't you? God knew what he was doing when he made woman from the man's rib. We are here because God knew that you would need us, so just accept the inevitable," she grinned as she patted his cheek.

When they'd gotten outside, they went their own separate ways with a promise to see each other later. "I have a meeting at 8:30 tonight, but I'll see you about 4 o'clock, if all goes well this afternoon," Cory said as he was giving her a peck on the cheek. He strolled toward his office while she almost ran back to the bank. She has to turn in her resignation. She has too many other things to do to spend time working.

Promptly at 2 o'clock, Donna brought Craig's parents to Cory's office. "Hello, Mr. and Mrs. Norton, it was so good of you to give me some of your time this afternoon, but I hope you'll understand shortly why I needed to talk to you as soon as possible. Won't you please have a seat?" He went to his desk, sat down and waited until he thought they were ready to listen. "You have lived here for quite awhile, I believe, so you know a lot of the people. I'm sure you've heard about the burglaries that happened a few weeks ago. I'm told that caused a good sale on dead locks."

"Yes, we sold a lot of them," Mr. Norton replied cautiously.

"Well, those home burglaries were not the only stealing that was taking place during a few rough days. A young man, who had his heart set on college, had worked all summer saving to pay for his tuition. He was foolish not to put it in the bank, but he trusted all the people in this town as we all had. One night he went to put his week's earnings in his room and found the money gone. He became so upset that he decided if someone could take from him then he would take from someone else, and he committed burglaries before he stopped to realize what he had done and came to me for advice. You know this young man very well, and your son, Craig, is a good friend of his brother."

"Are you saying that you're accusing Craig of having something to do with that money disappearing? I'll have you know that we've taught all our children to be honest, not to steal, and that you must earn what you get in life," Mr. Norton exclaimed emphatically.

"I'm sure you have, Mr. Norton, but sometimes the temptation is stronger than our will power to do right, especially when it is right in front of our eyes."

"Craig didn't take that money! We would've known if he had any money around the house! I just can't imagine him keeping something like that to himself."

"Calm down a minute, Harry," Mrs. Norton spoke up. "Do you remember the night I mentioned that Craig was acting sort of strange? He came home and went straight to his room instead of his usual checking the refrigerator or the cupboard for something to eat, and I noticed an odd look on his face. Well, the next morning when he came down to the kitchen, he was ready to leave even though he'd never eaten his breakfast or taken his hand out of his jacket pocket. It was about 10 o'clock and I asked him why he was wearing a jacket when it was still so warm in October this year. He mumbled something about catching a cold and was chilly. I offered him an aspirin and he clumsily took it because he still kept his one hand in his pocket. He then left as if he were in a hurry. Oh Dear, what has our son done?"

"You're wrong, Dear, our son wouldn't do something like that."

"Mr. and Mrs. Norton, I'm sorry but we know that Craig opened an account at the bank for a sizable sum. Do you have another explanation of where he could've gotten that kind of money?"

They both shook their heads and Mrs. Norton was wiping tears from her eyes. "What do you want us to do?" Mr. Norton asked.

"Okay, he's only 15 years old and the Chief of Police has been working with us to make sure none of the involved will have a record because of this. The items that were taken from the homes are being returned without revealing any names, and he is going to recruit some volunteers from the school and vicinity to do community work for the next few weeks, or maybe even longer, such as shoveling snow off the sidewalks along Main Street, spreading sand on ice patches, and hanging the Christmas decorations on the poles, etc. Craig will be a volunteer, but only a few people will know why. He will be watched closely, however, and if he should slack his duties, he will pay a stiff penalty depending on the wishes of the Chief. But, what we need now is the return of the money so that Jason, who worked and saved it, can get enrolled in college and follow his dream for the future. Do you feel you can handle that without alienating your son, because we don't want to cause any friction in your family. If you'd prefer, the Chief or I can handle it? I learned something that I probably should keep my mouth shut about, but I think you should know that your son had good intentions for the money. I understand he wanted to buy a new TV for the family for Christmas."

"Well, we wouldn't have enjoyed a new TV if it was bought with stolen money. We'll see that Craig brings the money to you yet today, if possible. He will apologize to Jason, and he will also be a volunteer until the Chief feels he has learned his lesson. There most likely will be a thing or two that I'll add to his chores at home, too."

With a smile, Cory replied, "Don't be too hard on him, Mr. Norton, because knowing that you love him even though he's done wrong, will also make a deep impression on a boy his age. If you can accomplish it, Jason will be here at 8:30 tonight to see what we have been able to find out, and it would be great if all the differences could be straightened out soon and not given time to fester."

"We'll be here, Mr. Calhoun, with or without the money. It depends on when we find Craig and how late the bank stays open today. The apologies will be taken care of at least. Thank you for handling it so well, without a lot of publicity, and I apologize for yelling at you earlier."

"You're a good father and I wouldn't expect you to react any other way. I'll expect to see you and Craig tonight about 8:30, and thanks again for coming in so we could get this settled without anymore delay." He opened the door, shook hands with them as they left, and then exhaled a sigh of relief, but after he'd returned to his desk and had put his head in his hands, a big hearty chuckle came from the doorway. "Go away, Roger or Clayton, I've had about as much as I can handle of this case for a few hours, at least." He looked up as Roger sat down in the chair across from him with a big smile on his face.

"You've done a great job, Mr. Attorney. Those two or three boys will someday realize what you did for them and will look up to you like we do to Mr. Harrington. I also spoke to the Chief and he has already gotten the items returned, but he's going to talk to the owners of the house, where nothing was taken, just to assure them that the problem has been solved.

As Clayton, I saw Craig during lunch. He said he was going to tell his parents about the money and that he wanted to return it to its rightful owner. He couldn't give me any of it and wished I would leave him alone. I felt so proud of him I almost took him in my arms for a hug, but I realized I was Clayton and had to act a little put out that I wasn't going to get a share of that money." Chuckling, he then waited for Cory to speak.

"Well, that should make it much easier for Mr. and Mrs. Norton who are on their way to find him and drag him to the bank. They will be here tonight with the money, if they can get to the bank before it closes, or at least to apologize to Jason and promise its quick return. It was hard for them to accept the fact that their son would do something like this because he had been taught, along with the rest of their children, right from wrong. I do owe you a lot, Roger, because you carried a big part of the load, and I do hope you know how much I appreciate it. You have certainly become a great friend after scaring Andrea and me half to death with your weird Clayton act, and we hope you'll be able to spend a lot of time here,"

"If Grace has her way, we'll live here permanently, and I'll get to stay in a hotel when I go to Boston on business. It really is amazing how things work out, isn't it? Well," he said, as he stood up to leave, "I think I'll go home and see how my little mama is feeling and I'll see you tonight a little before 8:30. Don't go getting tangled up with Andrea now and forget your duties," he laughed as he strolled out the door.

*Not much chance of that, but I do need to encourage her to think about a wedding date. Right now, though, I have just enough time to do an errand before I go see my cute playful wild tigress.*

Andrea had just gotten home and was changing clothes when he arrived, so he went to the kitchen and got the coffee brewing. He was ready to relax with some snacks and to snuggle up with his sweetheart. He'd pulled some cheese and grapes out of the fridge and found some crackers in the pantry by the time Andrea joined him. "Hello, My Baby, Hello, My Honey," he crooned as he swept her into his arms. "You're so sexy in those jeans," he teased as his hands dropped down and cupped her hips and then quickly ducked as he knew she would be swinging at him. He grabbed her fist, opened it up so he could kiss her palm, and then headed for her lips.

"How did things go with Mr. and Mrs. Norton?" she asked when they were settled on the couch.

"The case is closed except for the final exchange of the money along with apologies later this evening."

"That's good because we have some plans to finalize. Did you mention to Roger, by any chance, that we'd like to have them over here for Thanksgiving dinner? And, what about your mother and Sissy—have you called them? And tell me, please, what is her real name, Cory? I can't call her Sissy just because you do."

"I did talk to Roger about Thanksgiving, and he thinks it sounds wonderful and that Grace will be thrilled and want to help. No, I haven't talked to Mom and Sissy yet because I haven't had the time. I'll do that the first thing tomorrow morning. I think Sissy's real name is Sylvia, but you won't get to call her that," he chuckled as he ran his fingers slowly through her long silky hair. "Did I answer all of your questions, or are there more?"

Giving him a slap on the arm, she remarked, "It's just that Thanksgiving is only about three weeks away, and I'll bet you haven't the slightest idea what tonight is."

His mind was whirling as he tried to remember what the date was and suddenly knew what she was referring to. "Halloween," he said triumphantly, "and that is why I saw all that candy in the pantry when I was looking for these crackers. What time do the little monsters start coming?"

"You cheated because you saw the candy. Men never remember important dates on their own. Just another reason God made women. Will you be here to help me pass out the treats? Between 6 and 8:30, I think."

"Do they really play tricks on you if you don't give them a treat?"

"I doubt if any of the little ones even know what the word 'trick' means. They just want the candy and maybe a remark about their outfit, but I usually wear a mask and costume just to see their surprised faces when I open the door."

"Okay, I'll be here until 8:00 at least, but there's something else I'd like to talk to you about, Sweetie, and that is when can we get married? I was wondering if maybe we could elope right after Thanksgiving. We could go to Las Vegas and get married, and I'll find a neat place to go for our honeymoon. Would you consider doing that?"

"I'm still not sure that I know you well enough," she smiled teasingly, "but I have been thinking about it. No, I don't want to elope. I'd much rather talk to our Pastor and see if he could marry us in the church some Friday or Saturday afternoon before the weather gets too bad. I'm sure your mom and sister would drive down for your wedding, and Roger and Grace could be our attendants. Then we could fly down to one of those warm Caribbean islands to spend as much time as you can be away from the office. How does that sound to you?"

"Are you really serious, Honey? I thought I'd have to get down on my knees again and beg you to set a date. When do you think we could see the Pastor?"

"Well, if this case is wound up tonight and you have some time, we could try to catch him tomorrow afternoon, when I get off work."

"That's a date, Sweetheart," he said, imitating Bogart, as he pulled her into his arms and gave her a kiss that made her whole body react in a way she hadn't felt before.

She knew she wanted more than kisses, but she was also determined to wait until her wedding day, so she moved away from him. *I guess the date should be set,* she thought as she realized she was shaking. Do—do you want me—me to fix an er-early dinner so—so we can e-eat before the little one-ones start com—coming?" she stammered.

"Am I really starting to get to you, Andrea?" he grinned. "Why don't we just enjoy these snacks for now and then we'll go to the cafe after my meeting tonight? Does that sound all right?"

"That sounds fine. How about a grape?" she asked as she put one to his lips. Time flew by and about 5:30 they got masks from her ample supply and found outfits to match. He decided to be Zorro and she was the wicked witch. They were ready when the first little one arrived for a Trick or Treat.

He left at 8:10 to go to the office for the meeting. A couple of minutes later Roger arrived. However, they got quite a surprise when Jason showed up at 8:20 with his brother, Sam, in tow. "My brother knows something about what happened to my money, but he won't talk to any of us at home. I thought maybe you could get him to tell you what he knows."

"It's all straightened out, Jason, so we don't need Sam's explanation unless he wants to share it with us. We have someone coming shortly and everything will be cleared up. You are getting your money back, and we'll discuss what lies ahead for all three of you who have been involved. I don't believe it would hurt Sam to do some community work if he stood by and let this happen and wouldn't speak up to help his own brother and family. Do you want to say something, Sam, or do we wait for Craig and his father to arrive?"

"Mr. Norton and Craig are coming here?" Sam looked a little frightened, a little amazed, and a little skeptical all at once, and started for the door.

Roger was there to block his way, however, and said, "I don't think it's time for you to leave quite yet, Sam, and maybe you've got a bigger lesson to learn than Craig. Would you like to tell Mr. Calhoun, your big brother and me what part you played in all this, or would you rather tell it to the Chief of Police?"

"The Chief of Police knows about Jason's money?" With big tears welling up in his eyes, Sam told them how he had shown Craig the money that Jason was saving for college, but he never dreamed that Craig would steal it. "When Jason found it missing, I confronted Craig and learned that he'd put it in a savings account at the bank. Craig made me promise not to tell anyone or he'd make me very sorry. I didn't know what he would do to me or my family because he's a lot bigger than I am, so I felt I had to keep quiet."

At that moment, the door opened and Mr. Norton and Craig came in. Craig looked at Sam and had an apologetic look on his face. "I'm sorry, Sam, for all the trouble I've caused you and your family. You just showed me the money because you were so proud of your brother for earning it to go to college, and I took advantage of your friendship. Jason, I don't know how to apologize to you because I can't imagine how you felt when you found all your money gone, but I'm very sorry for what I did. The worst, or maybe the best, part of all of this was when I realized how many eyes were watching my every move. I certainly learned that you can't get away with doing wrong, especially when a really odd looking guy came up to me one day and tried to make me share with him. I'd seen him around town a few times and he reminded me of some hobo who had jumped off a train. He was really weird, but he sure got me to thinking, too.

Dad and I went to the bank this afternoon, and I want to give you your money back, Jason. It's all there, plus just a little I added of my own because I thought you deserved some compensation for having to go through this night mare. You might want to know that it would have gained some interest for you all summer if you'd put it in a savings account. I like that kind of stuff and would like to study to be a CPA or even a Stockbroker if I get to go to college. I'm sorry, Mr. Calhoun, I understand you have some things to talk to us about."

Cory looked at Roger, who could hardly keep from laughing out loud as he was being described, and Cory couldn't help but smile as he'd listened to the fluent explanation coming from the lips of this young 15 year old boy. He felt he had a great future ahead of him, whatever field he chose. He proceeded to tell them what the Chief had planned for their punishment and how very few would know they were serving time, so to speak, for this episode that had caused so much pain to several families. They would be hearing from the Chief when he had the other volunteers recruited and just how long they worked would also be decided by the Chief. After thanking Mr. Norton and Craig, he asked if Jason and Sam would stay for just a few more minutes.

"Boys, I won't keep you long, but I know your dad is handicapped from an accident on the job and that your mother works outside the home to help make ends meet. Is there anything your father could do if he had special equipment? Can he use a computer so he could do work at home, for instance? If he was in construction, I was just wondering if he could take off and figure material lists for home building, or other listings like that. Do you know what his expertise is in?"

"Dad took courses on home building and drew several house plans for the contractor he was working for before he was hurt. He got so depressed, though, that he wouldn't even talk to his boss so he wasn't asked to do anymore. Recently, he has mentioned he wished he had a drawing table and supplies so he could advertise and maybe get some work from people wanting to remodel or build new homes. He also mentioned that if he could afford a computer, he could set up a web site for advertising. Of course, his disability checks and Mom's work doesn't leave anything for extras like that."

"Thanks, boys, for coming tonight. Jason, you know where to go tomorrow with that money, right? Do you have a safe place to keep it tonight?"

"I was going to ask if you would be willing to keep it for me until tomorrow. I have to work from 8:00 until 2:00 and then I'll take it to the bank. Could you keep it for me until then?"

"I'd be most happy to do that, Jason, and I want to talk to you some more anyway. Let me put it in the safe here and I'll see you shortly after 2:00 tomorrow. Do you two need a ride home?"

"Oh, No, we'll be fine. Thank you so much for all you've done. I'll pay you your fee out of the money before I take it to the bank."

"We'll figure that out tomorrow. Be careful going home. Sam, it's been nice meeting you and I hope you've learned, by going through this experience, that there are some things families keep to themselves. I'll be seeing you around, I'm sure, and don't hesitate to stop in and see me if you need someone to talk to. I'm certainly glad Jason knew where to come when he needed help. Goodnight, now."

When the boys were outside the door, Cory turned to Roger and smiled. "Well, do you think we made a little difference in the lives of those three boys, Partner?"

"Yeah, as I told you earlier, I think those boys will look up to you the rest of their lives as we will to Mr. Harrington. I am really thrilled that I got to play a small part in the scheme, and I loved hearing myself being described and now know that I made a difference.

However, I don't understand the questioning about their dad. Are you having some thoughts about helping the whole family? If you are, I want to be in on it. After all, their mother is our cleaning lady."

"Okay, Roger, you take care of your cleaning lady and let me handle these thoughts I'm having about helping their dad. Thanksgiving and Christmas are coming, and a real nice bonus would be a nice gesture. Right now, let's head out of here and go see our pretty ladies. I told Andrea that we'd go to the cafe for a bite to eat after I was through here. Would you and Grace like to join us?"

"We might just do that. For the past week, Grace is usually ready for another snack about this time of night," he chuckled. "I'll check with her and see if she feels like coming down the hill. She may already be in her pajamas, though, since we're leaving early in the morning. If not tonight, we'll see you when we get back. Goodnight, Cory."

"Until later, Roger, and thanks again for your help."

*Chapter Twelve*

When Cory reached the cottage, he found Andrea curled up on the couch, covered with an afghan and almost asleep. "Wake up, you sleepy head, Get up, Get out of bed," he sang as he yanked the cover off and pulled her to her feet. "All's well and it's time to eat." He'd gotten her coat as he came through the foyer and now wrapped it around her as he pulled her into his arms for a kiss. "Roger is going to see if Grace feels up to joining us before they leave for Boston in the morning."

"That's nice," she remarked as she gave a big yawn. "Sorry, the program I had on was rather boring, but I couldn't find anything else I wanted to watch either."

"Do you want to walk to the cafe and wake up with the nice fresh air in your face?"

"Yes, let's do. We can pretend we're trick or treating and leave treats on all the porches. I have a lot of candy left." She got a box of small plastic bags from the kitchen and her bags of candy and off they went. They deliberately let the packages slide into the doors so the noise could be heard inside the house, and then they ran and hid behind a tree to see if anyone came to the door. They ran out of houses before they ran out of candy so they gave to people they met on the street and took the rest into the cafe. Luckily, it was still rather busy so they finally exhausted their supply of Halloween candy.

Roger and Grace were sitting in a corner booth watching the proceedings with big smiles on their faces. "I hope you two never grow old because it's a blast watching you," Roger remarked as Cory and Andrea joined them. "Grace, I'd like you to finally meet the Miss Andrea Harrington, the one who orders all of us handsome men out of her house. Andrea, this is my wife, Grace. Please be gentle with her because she's carrying a future bundle of joy for me in her belly, but right now she's trying to decide what this sixth meal of the day should consist of," he chuckled.

"Oh, Roger, it's not that bad yet. Just wait until your heir really starts growing," she laughed. "Andrea, I'm so glad to finally meet you face to face. I must say I've enjoyed the last three months wondering what Clayton was going to face next trying to carry out your father's instructions. But, isn't it wonderful what these two guys have accomplished in our little town the last few days? Those young boys are so lucky."

"You're so right, Grace, but I haven't heard all that happened at the meeting tonight. I guess Cory and I got carried away with the candy," she giggled and then looked at Cory for some information.

"I'd rather tell you later where it's not so public," he whispered in her ear and then kissed her cheek. "Let's talk about more important things, like Thanksgiving and what's following that." He gazed at her with love glowing in his eyes.

Holding his gaze, she smiled as she nodded and then turned to address Roger and Grace. "I understand that Cory has spoken to Roger about the Thanksgiving dinner I would like to prepare and have the two of you and Cory's mom and sister as my guests. Do you think you'll be here and could join us?"

"We'd be very happy to come, but I'd want to help with something. What could I bring that would help you the most?"

"Just so I don't ask you to bring something you don't particularly like to fix, is there anything you like to make which would be easy in your delicate condition?"

"I do have a cranberry salad recipe that I got from a college friend's mother that I like to make and you can make it ahead of time. I also like to make pecan pies. Would either or both of those help you?"

"Oh, Grace, I'd love both of them, but I hate to ask you to bring that much. I wasn't expecting you to bring anything."

"No problem, Andrea, and I'll check with you when we get back from Boston."

"What about the other event, Sweetie? Don't you want to ask them about that?" Cory had his long lashes fluttering as his smile spread across his face.

"We don't know for sure about that, Cory, so let's wait until they get back from their trip to Boston. We have some things to discuss and decide on before anything can happen."

"Oh, oh," Roger chuckled as he looked from one to the other. "Do I sense a visit to the pastor coming soon? We'll be thrilled to be attendants, if that's the occasion. It sounds like a great time for a wedding with Cory's mom and sister in town.

Come on, you guys, don't keep us guessing—tell us, are you going to tie the knot around Thanksgiving?"

"Roger, that's not nice," Grace scolded him. "Let them tell us when they're ready and have the details worked out. You realize we don't know each other too well and maybe they have others they want to ask. It was out of line for you to offer our services."

"Thanks, Grace, you're an angel. Nothing is for sure yet, and Cory should not have brought it up." Andrea gave him a look that could've made a turtle pull its head back into its shell real fast, and Roger and Grace couldn't help but laugh.

Somehow, orders had been given to the server and she was now bringing their food to the table. The conversation flowed from one subject to another and they had a great time although the time passed too quickly.

Roger and Grace were wished a safe trip as they went the opposite direction from Cory and Andrea when they were outside the cafe.

When they reached the cottage, Cory built a fire in the fireplace while Andrea fixed them cups of hot tea which they enjoyed after their brisk walk home. He also told her about the earlier meeting with Jason, Sam, Mr. Norton and Craig, and Andrea was so thrilled when he finished that she gave him a big hug and kiss. "Knowing your connection with my father, I'm sure you have a plan in that head of yours for delivering a TV to the Norton home, plus getting an assortment of supplies to Mr. Anderson. Are you going to let me be a part of it?"

"You may be getting to know me quite well, Miss Harrington, but that means your excuse for putting off our wedding date because you don't know me well enough is also a little more feeble," he said as he reached over to run his fingers through her hair that she had pulled back into a pony tail tonight. He then tugged on it until she fell back against his chest.

"I've agreed to talk to the pastor, Mr. Calhoun, so don't try to change the subject now. Why can't you just tell me what you're going to do and let me decide if I can help you or not? Don't go being an egotist."

"Whoa, My Little Tigress. Before this comes to blows, let me remind you that you're quite a bit like your father, but, as many of his traits were very good, there may be some that are not so good in your case. One thing you'll have to learn, Andrea, is the fact that I'm an attorney, my cases are my responsibilities and I'll be the one handling the decisions I make. You'll stay out of them unless I ask you for help or input. Do you understand, Sweetie? Any other way could cause irreparable repercussions in my work as well as our relationship."

"Well, if that's the way you feel, Cory, I think it's time for you to leave. Just get out of here so I can decide how I want my future—with or without you. GOODNIGHT!" She was tromping off to her bedroom, and he sat there smiling and shaking his head. *What a life I'm letting myself in for.*

Andrea was sobbing by the time she'd reached her bed and thrown herself across it. *Why does he always have to be right? I know I shouldn't get involved in his cases, but I really want to help with this one. I know the Norton family—they're even using some of my old furniture, for Heaven's sake. They apparently need a new TV, and I know Cory is going to see that they get one, but how?*

As Cory sat there, he realized he'd been at fault, too, because he shouldn't have told her all the details if he didn't want her to get involved. He should have known she would want to help, but there has to be some way for them to be amicable. He got up and strolled toward her bedroom, stopping at the door. He could see her lying across the bed so he slowly inched closer, sat on the edge of the bed and reached over to massage her back.

"Why are you still here?" she asked through her sniffles.

"Will you talk to me, Sweetheart?"

She rolled over on her side so she was facing him and whispered, "I'm sorry, Cory. I know I can't intrude on your cases. It was just that this one involved families I know and I didn't think about it as being a case. I'll try to remember my place, and when I forget, you'll have to remind me again. Will you forgive me?"

"Of course, Andrea, and I want to apologize, too. I didn't have to sound so high and mighty, but I think if we can resolve all our differences as easily as this one, we will do just fine." His massaging continued and she was soon purring like a kitten. He removed her shoes and socks and then her sweat pants and zippered top. *We both must sleep soundly,* he thought, as he pulled the covers back just enough so he could slip her under them. He bent to kiss her cheek, checked the fireplace and doors, and then went to the other bedroom. *I should go home, but I never want to leave you, Andrea, and I want to get married. Please, God, let our wedding be soon.* He suddenly felt God's presence as he fell asleep.

Andrea awakened the next morning and immediately glanced over to the other side of the bed to see if Cory had slept beside her again. She found herself a little disappointed that no one was there, but she could smell coffee and bacon. She had thrown the covers back and sat up on the side of the bed before she realized she was clad only in her bra, panties, and T-shirt. Remembering the soothing massage but not getting undressed, her thoughts went a bit crazy. *Cory must have undressed me last night, but what else did he do?* She was shaking as she quickly grabbed her robe, slid her feet into her fuzzy slippers, and then went stomping toward the kitchen.

"Good morning, Sweetheart," Cory turned from the stove with a big smile on his face, but he stopped short when he saw her expression. It was flushed with anger.

"Don't good morning me, Cory Calhoun. Why did you undress me last night and just what did you do to me?" Starting to whimper and stammer, she asked, "Cory, did yu-you, did yu-you do some-something to m-me last ni-night while I-I slept?" She started toward him with a fist clinched ready for a fight, but hesitated when she saw that he was smiling, his eyes were sparkling, and he was also chuckling. "Oh, what are you smiling about, you man?" she snapped as she stomped over to the table, pulled out a chair and sat down rather hard and then just stared at him.

"Now, Andrea, Darling, just calm down." While his smile grew a little bigger and his chuckling grew a little louder, he remarked, "If I had done anything to you last night, Andrea Harrrington, you would *not* have slept through it, of that you can be sure. After my massage put you to sleep again, I just thought you'd be more comfortable if you didn't have that heavy sweat suit on, but I left you covered with your rather long T-shirt and panties. What's so wrong with that? . . . I didn't see as much of you as I saw of those girls who wore the skimpy bikinis this past summer, especially out on the boats."

"I don't wear bikinis," she replied still rather angrily. "As a matter of fact, I wear one piece swimsuits because that's what Dad preferred, but that's not the problem we're actually discussing here. You undressed me. Did you sleep beside me again, too?"

"No, I didn't, Andrea. Would you have liked me to?" he chuckled as he ambled over toward her now with his arms at his sides. "Are you about ready to admit that I'm getting to you?" he asked as he knelt beside her, his arms quickly slipping around her and pinning her arms against her body as he pulled her into a tight embrace.

"You are not getting to me, Mr. Calhoun. I'm just trying to figure out if I want this relationship or not. It wasn't my plan at all, you know, that my father picked you to be his attorney or that he picked you to give me security and whatever else he thought you could give me. I'm very capable of taking care of myself."

"Are you trying to convince me or yourself, Miss Harrington? You seemed to really appreciate the fact that I was around when you thought Clayton might come walking in on you again, and I don't think you were too upset yesterday morning when I was beside you when you awoke, even though I was on top of the covers and you were beneath them. In fact I thought you rather enjoyed the extra little bit of kissing we shared," he chuckled as he lifted her chin so he could look into her gorgeous blue eyes. "Why do you want to keep fighting our getting married when you know you'd be lost without me?" he grinned as he fluttered his long eyelashes which, of course, made her heart thump so that all she wanted to do was hold him, yes, hold him tight and never let him go.

"I don't know, Cory, maybe I'm afraid that I don't know enough about relationships to make it work. I certainly haven't had any experience with a serious affair before, and it is really scaring me. I want my marriage to last the rest of my life, but I've seen several of my friends get divorces and feel so disillusioned. I'll admit I've felt this special closeness to you, but how do I know it will last?"

"Love is what will keep our world together, Sweetheart, and also create a bond or a relationship that will withstand all the problems and disappointments, while giving a lasting excitement and joy about all the many wonderful events of marriage."

"But we haven't known each other long enough, Cory, to know whether we'll be compatible or not. You don't know how I feel about, ah . . . well . . . politics for example, and I don't know what your likes and dislikes are about, ah . . . food, furniture, and fitness," she tossed out rapidly.

"And you are grasping at straws, Andrea, because you are apprehensive about an unknown adventure. But we do know a lot about each other . . . you know that I'm a very good attorney who loves to help others, I know how to handle a boat, I can install dead bolt locks, and I have adorable eyelashes that makes your heart thump whenever I flutter them. You know I have my mom and my sister; that I don't snore, I give great massages, and I can also fix coffee, bacon and eggs.

I know that you are good at handling money, you have a quick temper but then almost always ready to take the blame and make up, you are a wonderful cook and you are great at teaching the techniques of maneuvering a boat. You are willing, even anxious to help others, and that you are looking forward to having morning sickness more than once. And, you love me and are as anxious for me to make love to you as I am to return the favor. There are so many couples who know much less about one another before they get married."

"And you, Cory Calhoun, know exactly how to make me wish our wedding was going to be tomorrow."

"Which reminds me, Sweetie, do you want me to contact Pastor Avery and see when he can talk to us, or do you want to do that?"

"I think that falls on the bride-to-be's do-it list, so I'll call him this morning and let you know what he says. Now, can we eat before everything is completely cold or burnt?"

Bowing deeply, Cory smiled as he said, "At your service, Ma'am."

The appointment was made for 4:30 with Pastor Avery, and Andrea went to Cory's office, after she left work, so they could go to the church together. She couldn't shake her nervousness, but she knew in her heart that this was what she wanted to do. The meeting went well, and the date was set for Saturday afternoon, November 25th, at 3 o'clock. She'd asked if the organist would be available, and remarked that she would also like to have a soloist but didn't know any personally.

Cory spoke up, "I know one, Andrea, and she'll be at the wedding. My sister has a beautiful voice, sang in the A Cappella Choir in High School, was also a member of the College Chorus and now sings in her Church Choir. She'd be so thrilled if she could sing at our wedding. Just tell me the song or songs you want her to sing. She and Mom can plan to come early enough for her to practice with the organist, if that is possible, or she can sing without accompaniment."

"That's one more thing I know now about you and your family," she whispered as she gave him a big smile.

"Do you think you'll need a rehearsal on Friday night, Andrea?" the Pastor asked. "A small wedding is usually quite informal, but if you've not been in many weddings and would like to have a little practice, it can certainly be arranged. I'll go ahead and confirm the date with the organist and she'll probably contact you on the choice of music and also when she can meet with Cory's sister. May I have her name, address, and phone number to give to the organist?"

"Certainly, it's Sylvia Calhoun, but better known as Sissy," Cory volunteered. "She and my mother live in Quincy but will be here several days before Thanksgiving." He was explaining this as he was writing down the phone number and address for him.

"What do you think, Cory? Do we need a rehearsal?" Andrea asked.

"I think we should take 30 minutes or so and talk through the procedure, at least, if the church will be available. It would probably help things run more smoothly Saturday."

"That's fine. Could you come about 4:30 on Friday, the 24th, and we'll take a few minutes to go through the normal happenings, Your attendants will need to be here, too."

"Yes, we'll make arrangements for them to come with us," Cory answered.

After a few more questions and answers, they were ready to leave. "Thank you so much, Pastor Avery, for meeting with us on such short notice, and we'll look forward to seeing you that Friday at 4:30," Andrea remarked as they reached the door.

When they were outside the church and heading for Cory's car, Andrea couldn't help from bouncing along like a little girl with a new doll. "Oh, Cory, doesn't it sound thrilling, and I can't believe that I'm lucky enough to have your sister sing at our wedding. Why didn't you ever tell me that your sister could sing?"

"Well, the subject of singing hasn't exactly come up for discussion before, Sweetie, but I'm sure you'll enjoy hearing her. Do you have any favorite wedding songs you'd like to have sung? She has almost all the old favorites and quite a few popular ones that the jet set likes to use."

"No, I don't want any of those current ones that are hard to understand where they are going with the words. I like the old favorites like "I Love You Truly" or "Because" plus I've always loved the singing of "The Lord's Prayer" as the bride and groom kneel in prayer. I also want the Unity Candle that we light together to represent our forming a new family."

"That sounds really great, Sweetheart. Would you like for Sissy to sing both of the songs that you mentioned, maybe one just before you start down the aisle and the other after the opening remarks? Why don't I talk to Sissy and see what her thoughts are on the subject? Maybe you'd feel comfortable letting her select the songs. Think about that, okay? But, how about going somewhere and getting something to eat now? I'm starved."

"Sounds good to me, Mr. Calhoun. You're driving, so it's your choice."

"And so it is, my soon-to-be bride, and you can't change your mind about marrying me now that we have the church reserved."

"Oh, I've heard about some run-away brides, but I don't want to become a national news story so I guess I'm ready to accept my fate," she giggled. "I've been thinking, Cory, about your suggestion of letting Sissy pick the songs, and that's a pretty good idea. She'd know which ones she likes to sing, and what has been used lately, but would you please tell her I don't want any of those that have no rhyme or rhythm?"

"I'll be happy to do that, Sweetie, and she'll get your approval before it's confirmed with the organist."

"Oh, that's right. Everything is going to be perfect for our wedding, I just know it."

"It couldn't be anything but perfect when you're going to become my bride."

>>                                                                      >>

## Chapter Thirteen

About 10 o'clock Friday morning Cory was sitting at his desk studying a document that Donna had just finished typing for him. He thought he heard the front door open, but then there was complete silence. *Where is Donna?* he wondered. *Did she slip out to do an errand without telling me?* He had started to stand as he listened quietly for some sound or movement, but then a figure appeared at his door. Startled, he looked up but then yelled, "Marshall Walker, you old Sonofagun, what are you doing down in my neck of the woods?"

He rushed to give his old friend from the Boston Law Office a hug. "I didn't think anyone would ever wander down here just to see me, so what's on your mind? Did Donna see you? Oh, I get it now. You hushed her up. Come on in here and sit down so you can tell me how life's been treating you. I'm sure it's been hard since Jaylene died."

"It has been pretty rough the last sixteen months, Cory, and I guess I tried too hard to smother my grief in work. Recently I realized I'm just burned out and I want to find a place where I can slow down, work a little, but also be able to relax. Maybe I'll buy a boat so I can fish and get a tan, and if I'm real lucky, I may even find me a sweet young lady to marry. It's definitely too lonely to keep living by myself. That's the reason I'm here, and I'm wondering if you can help me out."

"Anything, Marsh, that I have the power or ability to do, you know that. You were the one I most hated to leave when I came here. Did you hear that Mr. Harrington passed away in June?"

"Yes, it was in the Boston papers, of course, and a small part of his estate leaked into the financial news, as well. Sounds as if he did quite well for himself. I assume you've met his daughter by now, so what is she like? I remember your remarks about how much he talked to you about her—all those flattering descriptions—until you were hoping you'd never have to meet her. Did she live up to his descriptions?"

"Oh, yeah, Marsh, she certainly did, and I remember my thoughts all too well. Now I wish I could take them all back. Mr. Harrington tried several times to get me to meet her but I always came up with an excuse. If I had only let him introduce us, then he could have had the pleasure of walking his daughter down the aisle and giving her away, because I think I fell in love with her the moment I saw her. Although I had a little trouble convincing her, we are getting married the Saturday after Thanksgiving."

"Wow, Cory, that's a rather sad story but also a wonderful ending. Congratulations, I really envy you because there's nothing like a marriage to fulfill a man's life. Take it from one who knows."

"Well, you'll have to meet my Wild Tigress and judge for yourself how exciting and fulfilling you think my life is going to be, but from my point of view, it's going to be the most exhilarating time of my life."

Marshall was laughing at the beaming face of his friend and knew that he was one guy definitely in love. "I'm looking forward to meeting her and maybe also becoming your neighbor, because I'm looking at a cottage to buy about two blocks from hers. I saw the big Bluewater moored there and almost drooled. I hope Andrea's a good navigator, but I guess it really doesn't matter, does it, if you're getting married? You certainly know how to operate a boat, but what about the winterizing? It's getting a little cold, isn't it, for a boat to still be in the water?"

"That boat is already mine, Marsh, and there's a circulation system that is running. Andrea says it has worked well for the last two years. Mr. Harrington wrote a codicil to his Will which gave me the boat as well as a nice compensation for, as he stated, considerations I'd given him the past several years. Can you believe that after all that man did for me? But enough of that—tell me, what's this plan of yours for being here, especially if you're thinking about buying one of the cottages?"

"Well, I was hoping you might like to have a part-time attorney in your office. I don't really need a big income, Cory, but you know I would go crazy without something to do day after day, and you know how I love the law. I've felt God talking to me for some time now about slowing down, and you had been appearing too much in my thoughts and dreams to ignore the gentle push in this direction.

Hey, I just thought of something—you're going on a honeymoon, aren't you? Do you have anyone to keep the office open? Maybe you'd let me hold down the fort, along with Donna, while you're off making love on a warm Caribbean island or wherever. We could possibly work it out so we could both have time to pursue some interests outside the confines of the four walls. Would you at least give it some thought, Cory, because I'd like to proceed with the purchase of my new home before someone else snatches it, if you'll give me the opportunity to stay here?"

"You go right ahead and buy your new home, Marsh. I've been thinking for awhile now about trying to find a part-time partner so I'll be able to spend some quality time with Andrea, but I could never have found one who'd measure up to you or your experience. I can't understand you wanting to come to this little town that doesn't have a lot happening that needs attorneys, but it's been a great place to meet some wonderful people and the town has been growing. Maybe we'll be able to generate more business as time goes by. By the way, what are you going to be doing for Thanksgiving dinner?"

Shrugging his shoulders, he replied, "I had thought about going to the folks, but I may be moving if the realtor can move fast enough on my offer for the cottage. I have my house sold in Boston and will close on it November 30th, so I have to get all my things out before then. The buyers want to move in before Christmas. That's why I want to buy the cottage as soon as possible."

"Plan on spending Thanksgiving with us, will you? Mom and Sissy are coming, and a young couple, Roger and Grace

Dayton, that we met in a very unusual way. That's a story you'll have to hear sometime. I'm inviting Donna so you'll know most of the ones who'll be there. Please say you'll come, and we'll help you get moved in."

"If you're getting married on that Saturday, who is going to fix the meal? Is your mother coming to do the cooking?"

"No, Andrea is doing most of the cooking. Grace is bringing something, but Andrea loves to cook and is good at it. She wants to do this, and she was the one who suggested the date for the wedding so I'm sure she can handle it. Although I'm not sure she knows all the details of planning a wedding, we'll all be helping. Mom and Sissy are going to stay and keep an eye on the cottage while we're gone. They were going to help Donna with the office, too, but if you're going to be around, they won't have to worry about that. So, what do you say? Can we count on you to be here for Thanksgiving dinner and, of course, the wedding?"

"Sure, why not? I didn't tell you but my resignation was effective at the firm on November 1, so I'm as free as a bird. By the way, is Sissy still writing her novels? It'll be great to see her and your mom again."

"She's still writing. I think she has a contract for a book or two a year so it keeps her rather busy and out of trouble, I guess. I wish she had time to enjoy life a little more, but she seems happy with the traveling she does for promoting her books, and there are a few friends she sees now and then. Why don't you come with me now? We'll pick up Andrea at the bank and go get a bite of lunch. That way, you can meet her now so you won't be complete strangers on 'Turkey Day'."

Glancing at his watch, Marshall realized it was almost noon and his stomach had just started talking to him. He hadn't been able to eat much breakfast because he was so anxious to see Cory and find out if his future held any promise around here. Now, he feels he could eat, or even devour, a good big lunch. "Thought you'd never ask, but maybe I shouldn't intrude on your time with Andrea. Are you sure she won't mind?"

"She is very gracious, Marsh, and I'm pretty sure she won't mind. Of course, being a wild tigress, she will also let us know if she disapproves," he chuckled. She is so anxious to help people, a lot like her father, that I had to lay down some rules the other day or I may have found her running my office." He was laughing as he got his jacket and, with Marshall, headed for the door. "Oh, Donna, before everything slips my mind with this guy hanging around, Andrea and I want you to join us for Thanksgiving dinner and also for our wedding on Saturday, the 25th. Be sure to mark your calendar."

He really chuckled as he watched her gasp, then clap her hands and murmur, "It's about time, Cory Calhoun."

Andrea was thrilled when Cory introduced her to Marshall and told her about the loss of his wife, his buying the cottage, and their plans for the office. She couldn't wait to start asking questions, but everything she wanted to ask sounded too personal for a first meeting so she kept her mouth shut and just listened to the guys talk.

However, her mind was going at a rapid speed as she thought, *I know the cottage well that he is interested in. It just went on the market. One of my friends lived there during the time my parents and I came for the weekends. It's a lovely cottage, and it would make a nice home for him and perhaps a new wife. Oh, could he possibly be the answer for a husband for Sissy? Well, why not, he already knows her, she works at home so 'home' could be just about anywhere, and Cory's mother could have his apartment after he gets his things out of it. It would be most convenient for her to get where she needed to go in town, and, if she doesn't have a car, she'd be close to Cory, Marshall, or Donna at the office. If they were tied up and she needed a ride, she could always call Sissy or me. It's a perfect solution for our whole family, and for Marshall who needs a wife.*

"Andrea, you haven't been listening to Marshall and me, but you've had the cutest smile on your face. Would you like to let us in on what you've been thinking about?"

"No, I'd rather not," she whispered, "because it's something very personal that I have to get done. I apologize for not being very good company, but I really do need to go and do some errands. Would you please excuse me? I am so happy to have met you, Marshall, and look forward to seeing you again soon." She slipped from her chair and hurried out of the restaurant.

"She's usually not in a trance like that, Marsh. I'm sorry she didn't add at least a few of her thoughts to our conversation."

"You don't need to apologize, Cory. I could see the bride-to-be jitters, but I'll warn you that it doesn't get any better until you have her all to yourself after the wedding is over. She is a beauty, and I understand why you were captivated when you first saw her."

"I'm really looking forward to having her all to myself. It's going to be the thrill of my life when I make her my wife. She's

25 and hasn't had a serious relationship before—her father must have been very protective—so it's going to be a pleasure learning the art of love together, so to speak." He felt his face getting a little flushed, but hoped Marshall wouldn't notice.

But, of course, Marshall saw it and smiled, but then changed the subject by asking, "What about Sissy? Does she have a steady boyfriend, or does she keep all her emotions for the novels she writes? She is such a beautiful person, I'd hate to think all that beauty is being wasted on those fiction stories."

"That's something I've wondered about myself. She used to date in high school and college, but I haven't heard her mention anyone since. Mom hasn't said anything either, so I just don't know what her love life consists of."

"I may have to check that out at Thanksgiving," he chuckled. "Would you mind if I got to know your sister a little better?"

"Sounds good to me, and if anything comes of it, I'd be very happy to have you as a brother-in-law." All at once, he couldn't contain his laughter. *That's what my little match-maker was thinking about, so naturally she couldn't tell us. I wonder what she has up her sleeve. I'd better tell her that Marshall has plans of his own so she'd be smart to let him carry the ball in this situation.*

"I think your thoughts must be on other things, too, Cory, so we'd better get you back to the office. I'm staying at the motel outside of town, so you can reach me there."

"I was just thinking about something Andrea did, but O.K., I do have a client coming at 2 o'clock and I was going over those papers when I was so rudely interrupted earlier," he chuckled. "Maybe we could meet you later at the motel for dinner. I like their food and they have a nice dance floor, too."

"I'll look forward to it. Should we make it about 6:30?"

"That's great. We'll see you then."

❦

After his appointment was finished and the client had left the office, Donna came to his door and announced, "You have a young man named Craig Norton, who would like to see you, but only if you have time."

"Craig is here? Surely, show him in." *I hope nothing has gone wrong between the three boys or with the Chief's challenge to them that he doled out. There were only three other volunteers who came forward so the six have been working pretty regularly.*

"Hello, Mr. Calhoun," Craig greeted him as he came in with a big smile on his face. "I just wanted to drop by and thank you again for helping me correct my stupid mistake and to let you know that I've learned when you do the right thing, you may be rewarded beyond your wildest imagination. Our family is so thrilled with the new TV that we were selected to receive from the Appliance Store free of charge. That man has never done anything like that before so I'm thinking there might have been a reimbursement by someone. You, of course, would know nothing about anything like that, would you, Mr. Calhoun?" he asked as he lifted his eyebrows. Since there was no response, except a smile, he continued, "Whatever, I just want you to know how appreciative my family is of the generosity extended to us."

"You are an outstanding young man, Craig, and I appreciate your coming in. I do realize that you're only 15, but you have a great way of expressing yourself. Do you have any idea what you want to do after graduation?"

Frowning a little, Craig answered, "I've thought about a lot of things I would like to do, but they all need a college education to have much of a chance for success, so I don't dwell on them too much. Besides the CPA and Stockbroker positions I mentioned the other night, I've always loved English and would like to be an English teacher, a writer and orator, or maybe even a stage actor," he said with a grin.

"Any of those would be worthwhile careers, and I'd like for you to keep your focus on those goals. By concentrating extra hard on English and Math, any one of those could be a successful career. If you'll do that, Craig, arrangements will be made for you to go to college. To start with, there are always good scholarships available for both Teaching and English Majors, and I'll promise to personally see that all the rest of your needs are met."

Standing up at his desk, Cory extended his hand to the speechless Craig. "I'd like to keep in touch with you, Craig, so I can help with your future. For now, I hope your family has a great Thanksgiving. Also, if you'd like, you could attend a wedding on Saturday afternoon, the 25th, at 3 o'clock," he adds with a smile.

"Are you going to marry Andrea Harrington? I've seen you with her quite a few times. That's wonderful, Mr. Calhoun, because she's a great person, a lot like her father who did a lot for our family. Ah . . . , just how many of my family are you extending this invitation to?" he grinned. "They are all crazy about Andrea, totally admired Mr. Harrington, and now respect you very much."

Chuckling, Cory remarked, "You would make a very good negotiator, Craig, maybe you should consider Politics. You may inform your entire family that they are included in the invitation, if they wish to attend a very small wedding, but one filled with lots of love."

"Thank you, Sir, I appreciate that, but I've taken too much of your time so I'll get out of here and let you get back to your work. You have a nice Thanksgiving, too. Oh, just for the record, I had my birthday the other day so I'm now 16."

"A belated Happy Birthday, Craig. Thanks for coming by. I do have an errand I need to do before I close for the day. It's been a pleasure talking to you. Remember, my door is always open for you, so don't hesitate to come see me."

## Chapter Fourteen

Cory drove out to the new Electronics Store which had opened recently not far from the Do-It-Yourself Center on the outskirts of town. He wanted to see if the computer had been delivered to Mr. Anderson yet. A drawing had been instigated as a Grand Opening advertising tool, and with a little coaxing and financing from Cory, it just happened that Mr. Anderson had been one of 'two' grand prize winners.

They informed Cory that the computer had been delivered and installed today, but it was the hardest prize they had ever tried to give away. Mr. Anderson had insisted that he'd never entered the drawing so there must be some mistake. He'd finally relented when they told him that someone else must have entered his name, so they're sending a man over next week to help set up the Web Page and answer any more questions he might have.

Very pleased that it was now at the Andersons, Cory thanked him and then headed for the Hobby and Craft Store where Jason is working, hoping he could catch him before he left work. It was close since Jason was just getting in his old beat-up car when Cory pulled in beside him and honked. Jason was out of his car quickly, and Cory motioned for him to get in so they could talk.

"Mr. Calhoun, it's so good to see you. Are you going to start a hobby or do you just need to buy some candles or something?"

"Nothing like that, Jason. I was hoping to catch you before you got away because I have a favor to ask. Maybe I shouldn't have done it quite this way, but it's done now and I'm going to ask you to fib, just a little, to your father." Smiling and also chuckling a little, he told Jason about the drawing and the computer being delivered today. "All I want you to do is tell your dad that you put his name in the drawing because you remembered that he'd talked about how he might be able to find some work to do at home if he had a computer. Can you do that with a straight face?"

"You bet I can, Mr. Calhoun, but my family shouldn't take anymore from you than what you've already done for me and Sam. You wouldn't know that Sam is the same kid. He actually loves the work Chief Winters is assigning us and has been talking about how he'd like to own or at least work for a Landscaping Firm when he graduates."

"That really pleases me, Jason, and what have you decided about getting enrolled in college? Do you want to start second semester? We'll need to get busy, if you do, and find the one you'd like to attend."

"I've been thinking a lot about that, Mr. Calhoun, and I just don't think I like the idea of starting in the middle of the school year, so I've decided I'd like to continue working this school year and then be ready to start college next Fall. I'll have more money by then, too."

"That sounds good to me, Jason, and it actually helps me with another problem I am trying to find an answer to. Roger Dayton, whom you've met, and his wife are in Boston this week, and they're going to check on a drafting board and all the other items your dad would need for work as an architect. Hopefully, they'll be bringing them when they return this weekend or by Monday at the latest.

I need a way to get your dad to accept them without involving me or Roger, and with you continuing to work is just what I'm looking for. I'm wondering if this would work— you go home and when you learn that he won the computer, you'll act very excited. Then you can proceed to tell him about putting his name in the drawing and that for the past few months you've been ordering a few other items through the Hobby and Crafts Store. It was to be his Christmas present, but since he has the computer now, you'd like to give them to him early so he can try to find some work whenever he's ready. People may want to get the plans drawn so they'll be ready to start their building early in the Spring. Do you think he'll buy it?" *I sure hope he doesn't find out what I've done or I may have an enemy for life.*

"It sounds like a perfect plan, Mr. Calhoun, but I can't understand why you want to do this for us. We'll never be able to repay you for all you've done already."

"Don't worry about that, Jason. I had a lot of help in my life from Mr. Harrington, and I want to do something for others to continue in his footsteps. Let's just leave it at that, okay? Another thing I'd like to say, though, is that Andrea Harrington and I are getting married on Saturday, the 25th, at 3 o'clock, and if you'd like to come and see me get hitched to the most wonderful girl in the world, you are now invited to help us celebrate."

"Congratulations, Mr. Calhoun, that's wonderful and if I don't have to work, I'll be there. Ah, could I bring Sam with me. He talks about you all the time and I know he'd love to attend your wedding. We haven't been to one since our sister got married about two years ago, and he wasn't thinking about girls and weddings then," he laughed. "He and Craig both had birthdays recently, so they're the big, romantic sixteen year olds right now."

Cory smiled as he said, "You're both invited, Jason. The more the merrier to fill the little chapel pews. I'd better let you get home, though, to see what your dad is doing with his new computer," he chuckled, but he waited long enough for Jason to get to his car. He then started the engine, slowly hooked his seat beat, and put the car in gear, but that was just long enough for him to hear the sputtering and coughing of Jason's car before the motor finally turned over. *He's got to have some decent transportation to get to work and then to college. Maybe it can be a Christmas present.*

Before they went to meet Marshall at the motel for dinner, Cory filled Andrea in on the conversation he and Marshall had about Sissy. "After you left so hurriedly after eating lunch, I caught on to your mood, Sweetie, but I do think you can let Marshall take care of that phase of his life. He likes Sissy and plans to check things out on Thanksgiving, when he joins us for dinner," he added sheepishly. "It just may work, and I told him I'd welcome him as a brother-in-law anytime."

"What's one more plate at the table, especially when it makes an even number, but you weren't very discreet, were you?" she giggled. "I'm glad you know him so well that you can encourage the relationship, but will he still want to have a child or two?"

"He's only 32 or 33, if I remember correctly," he laughed, "which would make him almost the same age as Sissy. He and Jaylene were married right out of college, and he told me in one of our many conversations that they had been informed by her doctor, after she'd had a miscarriage, that she wouldn't be able to have children. I think they had only been married about two years and he'd really been disappointed, but they were so much in love they were able to fill their lives with each other for almost six more years. Of course, his whole future was cut short when she died of cancer sixteen months ago."

"Wow, that is so sad, endearing, but also very encouraging," she grinned devilishly.

"Andrea, as I mentioned before, let's leave that relationship for Marshall to work out. In fact, let's not dwell on Marshall, but let's see what we can do about the love we have for each other," he whispered as he pulled her into his arms and kissed her very passionately. "Will that suffice until we get away from Marshall later tonight, or would you like to try a new move or two right now? Of course, if we did that, we may not even go to see Marshall tonight," he chuckled and then fluttered his long captivating eyelashes.

"I'll try to control myself," she smirked.

When they met Marshall for dinner, he informed them that he'd decided to go back to Boston on Sunday and load his van with items that he didn't want to put in the moving van. "Hopefully, I can bring enough to get by for a week until the rest of the furniture arrives. My bid on the cottage was accepted this afternoon and the closing date was set for the 16th with the executor and Donna since you were already gone. I'll go through the cottage tomorrow to see what I want to have done, and I'll make arrangements for it to be done while I'm gone."

Cory was pleased he would be able to handle the closing before the wedding and his taking off on his honeymoon.

"Since it was an estate sale," Marshall continued, "all of the former contents have been removed and there are no restrictions on what I can do before the closing. I'll plan to be back by the 11th and spend some time with you at the office that next week, learning the office layout and schedules. I'll contract for the truck to bring my furniture on the 16th or 17th so I can be settled before Thanksgiving. There will still be three days that next week for further instructions before sharing Thanksgiving and then your wedding."

Cory had been coerced by Andrea to discreetly try to get a key from Marshall, just in case something should happen and they needed to get in, of course. Andrea had her own ideas, however, for why she needed the key. She had finished her employment at the bank as of today, and she wanted to make sure the cottage was spotless before any furniture was to be brought in.

*Of course, I have a Thanksgiving dinner to plan, but that's no problem. My problem is the wedding, an unknown world to me, and I need a plan so everything will be ready not only for Thanksgiving, but also for the wedding, a reception, and a dinner. I just added the reception when Cory informed me this afternoon that he had invited the Norton family and also Jason and Sam. Just how many more will walk into his office and be invited before the 25th?*

She had to giggle at his enthusiasm as she realized she would have done the same thing if she'd been in his shoes. *Wouldn't it be nice if the chapel was full? Maybe I should contact some of my sorority sisters and see if they would like to come. I guess I'd better go talk to Pastor Avery again. Maybe he knows of a wedding coordinator, or whatever they're called, who can help me. I'll do that the first thing Monday. Yes, that's definitely the thing I'm going to do.*

"Where have you been, Sweetie?" she heard Cory's voice as her thoughts came back to the present. "You've been off in a world all your own again, and what was the giggle for? Are you sure you aren't taking on too much with Thanksgiving and the wedding so close together? We can make other plans, you know. I don't want you a limp rag doll after all this is over," he chuckled.

"No, Cory, I'll be fine. I was just thinking about checking with the pastor, though, to see if he happens to know of a wedding coordinator who could help. Maybe I could give her my ideas and then she could help me get them put together.

I know a couple of my sorority sisters talked about their coordinator, so there must be such a thing."

"There definitely are wedding coordinators," Marshall chimed in. "Jaylene had one and I was so glad because it was a huge wedding. The coordinator made everything run so smoothly."

"That's a great idea," Cory remarked. "I've heard about wedding coordinators, but I'd never realized what their job was. I hope there's one in this little town." Then, as he glanced at his watch, he said, "I do think, however, that it's time to call it a night. Thanks, Marsh, for the dinner, which I'd intended to pay for, but maybe we can reciprocate when you get back next weekend. If there's anything we can do at this end, please give us a call. Do be extra careful with that back of yours when you're lugging boxes, and remember to drive carefully," he chuckled.

"Will do, My Son," he moaned as if his joints were old and feeble, "and if I can help at your wedding, please let me know."

"He'll be such a wonderful addition to the office," Cory remarked as he'd opened the car door for Andrea and then was headed back into town.

They had hardly gotten out of the parking lot before she asked, "Were you able to get a key from him?"

"No, Andrea, he's much too smart to fall for that one. He knew immediately what we, or you, were planning to do and he'd have no part of it. With Thanksgiving dinner and the wedding, he thought you had enough on your plate, and I agree."

*There's other ways to get into that cottage, and I wasn't planning to do all the work myself anyway. I swear Marshall is going to have a clean house to come back to.*

"Sweetie, there's something else I want to talk to you about, though. When I saw Jason today, I got a look at the car he's driving and also heard it trying to run. If he's going to work and then go to college, he's going to need better transportation than what he has now. Do you think I should buy him a car?"

She was very quiet for a minute, thinking, but then, with a big smile, she said, "I think it's wonderful, Cory, and I have an idea. I've never really liked my dad's Jeep, so why don't we give it to Jason and then I can buy the car I've been dreaming of for a long, long time. Hmmm? I'm sure most guys would love the Cherokee."

"You've never mentioned not liking the Cherokee before, so are you just trying to get involved in one of my decisions again?" He'd tried to make it sound like he was teasing, but he was afraid it hadn't come out that way, and he was so right.

"Look, you, you over-inflated, self-centered ah . . . ah . . . attorney, you were the one who asked me for an opinion, so don't get all high and mighty with me. If you really didn't want an opinion from me, why did you even talk to me about it? Just go do what you want and leave me out of it, and then I won't have to intrude on your precious decisions."

Since he'd just turned into her drive, she was out of the car and into the house before he got the engine turned off and the key out of the ignition. He jumped out and ran to the door, only to find it locked and, of course, she wouldn't come and let him in. After he had knocked until his hand was sore, he decided to go home and let her cool down.

*Man, I have to remember to get a key to this place or I may find myself sleeping in the car more often than I care to imagine, especially if I don't learn how to talk to her. If things should work out for Sissy and Marshall, Mom could take over my apartment and I'd hate for her to know I get locked out occasionally when I'd have to knock on her door.* He couldn't keep from laughing as he tried to imagine his mother's reaction to that scene.

Andrea threw herself on the bed and cried. She'd wanted to run to the door when Cory was knocking for so long, but her pride just wouldn't let her. She finally sat up and saw her Bible on the nightstand. Picking it up, it fell open to Proverbs 19. When she reached verses 13 and 14, she read, 'A foolish son is his father's ruin, and a quarrelsome wife is like a constant dripping. Houses and wealth are inherited from parents, but a prudent wife is from the Lord.'

She fell on her knees beside the bed and prayed, "Dear Jesus, the one who knew no sin while confronting all kinds of people and problems during your stay on earth, how can I grow to be tolerant of other's feelings and think before I react so foolishly. Cory is the love of my life and I want to be wise and understanding, but I guess being spoiled by my parents and pretty much having my own way hasn't exactly prepared me to submit to my husband as the Bible states in the 3rd chapter of Colossians. I ask that you help me, Lord, to control my temper and think a problem through before I act. In your name, I pray. Amen."

She read for awhile longer since she was too upset with herself to go to sleep. She'd even thought about calling Cory and apologizing, but she couldn't bring herself to do that, either. "I guess I'm going to need a lot more help before I can really become humble, Lord, but Cory has said he doesn't want to change me. Maybe I can try, though, to have a little extra patience with him and others and to control this quick temper of mine."

After a lot of tossing and turning, Andrea had finally fallen asleep around 3:00 a.m. so she wasn't in any hurry to get up Saturday morning, but of course, the phone had to start ringing around 10 o'clock. *No, Cory Calhoun, I'm not ready to talk to you yet. You can just take some time to figure out why I'm so upset with you.* As the phone continued to ring, however, she picked it up and answered, "It's your nickel."

After a slight pause, a lady's soft voice, sounding quite puzzled, said, "Andrea? This is Cory's mother. Is something wrong, Dear?"

"Oh . . . Mrs. Calhoun, I'm so sorry. I was expecting it to be a person with whom I'm a little upset right now. Everything is fine and it's nice of you to call. I'm really anxious to get the chance to meet you and Sylvia."

"Sissy will be very disappointed if you insist on calling her Sylvia, but maybe it'll be a little easier to call her Sissy after the two of you have met. Why I called, Dear, is about the sleeping arrangements when we get there. Cory insists that it will be okay for us to stay at his apartment and he'll stay at the cottage with you and sleep in your father's room. We don't want to inconvenience you when you'll have all those preparations to make for the dinner as well as the wedding, and according to the old rules, the groom isn't supposed to see the bride on the wedding day until you meet at the altar. Sissy and I would be willing to stay at the motel if it would make it easier. You just say the word, Andrea."

*Oh, how I'd love to say a lot of words, Mrs. Calhoun, about how your son is trying to rule my life after he assured me that he loves me just the way I am. But that isn't any of your concern. I'll handle your son in my own time and place.* "Whatever arrangements Cory has made with you, Mrs. Calhoun, will be fine. Do you know what day you're coming? Cory has neglected to mention an exact date. He did say that Sylvia has agreed to sing at the wedding and I'm elated. I'd be happy to make arrangements with the organist for a practice if I knew your schedule."

"Oh, that son of mine never did know how to relay messages. The organist has called us, Dear, and they are going to practice on Tuesday, the 21st. We're planning to go to church on the 19th and then drive down that afternoon, and hopefully we'll be able to help you with some of the details. Is there anything we can do before we come? It seems like so much to place on your shoulders."

"No, Mrs. Calhoun, everything will be fine. I love to cook so Thanksgiving dinner is no problem, and I'm going to see about a wedding coordinator on Monday so I'm hoping a lot of the details of the wedding will be done by her."

"Oh, I'm so glad to hear that. I was afraid it might not be possible to find one in such a small town. I'm sure that will be a big help to you. Well, Dear, I'll let you go, and we both are looking forward to meeting you. If you want to change any of the plans, please just let us know. Goodbye for now."

*Well, Andrea, that was a very good way to start a relationship with your future mother-in-law. When are you going to learn? Maybe you should just pack up and leave. Everyone would probably be better off.*

"Dear Jesus, I guess it's going to take more than one prayer for you to help me be the prudent wife I would really like to be. I'll keep trying if you'll stay by my side."

She heard the knocking on the door again, like she'd endured last night for some 20 minutes, and she knew he wouldn't give up this time. *I guess I might as well face him and get it over with. After all, I'm going to marry the guy and maybe it'll be like the old saying goes, making up is the better part of an argument.* When she got to the door, she glanced through the window, but when she saw only a huge bouquet of roses, she knew she couldn't resist the man carrying them. She opened the door, however, and with all the sarcasm she could muster, and said, "When are you ever going to ask for a key to this place?"

"Hi, Sweetie," he replied as he peeked around the roses, and then started laughing as he stepped inside. He took the roses in one hand, turned her around with the other, gave her a swat on her rump and said, "Go get some clothes on before I lose all the control I have left when I'm around you."

"Oh, not again," she grumbled as she scampered off to her bedroom to get out of her gown and put on some clothes. "How can you always manage to show up right after I've had a wake-up phone call that leaves me upset?" she called out to him.

"Who called you this time since Clayton isn't around? Oh, oh, did my mother happen to call you? She asked for your phone number the other day when I talked to her. I'm really sorry if she upset you, Andrea. Apparently it runs in my family."

"No, it wasn't anything she said, Cory. It was the way I answered the phone that was very disturbing to me, when I realized who was calling." As she came back into the living room, she continued, "I thought it would be you when the phone started ringing at 10 o'clock this morning, and after I let it ring several times, I answered by saying 'It's your nickel.' I'm sure you've seen the commercial about boo boo's people make and then there's this guy who asks 'Do you want to get away?' Well, that's exactly the way I felt when this sweet voice said, 'Andrea, this is Cory's mother.' I felt like running far, far away."

Cory couldn't help but laugh although he knew what she must've gone through at that moment. "I'm sure you made her feel very comfortable by telling her you thought it was someone you were upset with, like her son, right? Come here, you little devil, and tell me you forgive me for ruffling your feathers again."

She ran to where he was seated and got settled on his lap before his arms went around her and the kissing began. She was ready for it to last for hours and hours. *How lucky can one completely irrational person be,* she asked herself as she got lost in the exhilarating thrill of his closeness and the distinctive smell of his aftershave.

Time passed, and as he continued to hold her, cuddling, snuggling, and kissing, his hand had finally found the bottom of her sweater and inched its way to her midriff. She felt herself shiver at the touch and then moan as all those strange feelings were sweeping through her body again as his hand moved slowly upward toward her breasts. She stopped his hand as she pulled away so she could see his face and ask, "Cory, what do all these reactions to your touching me mean?"

"That you love me, Sweetheart, and you can hardly wait for the day of our wedding when you'll get to experience the whole exciting act of lovemaking." He then began to sing, "I'll lay you down and whisper sweet nothings in your ear, lay you down and tell you all the things a woman wants to hear, and then I'll get to lay you down and love you thoroughly, and that will be the greatest day for me." He pulled her sweater up just enough so he could easily kiss her midriff.

"I wish I'd listened to my sorority sisters more closely as they talked about their dates and what they liked and disliked about them," she giggled and then shivered as he kissed her flat little stomach. She then gasped as she realized he'd managed to get his hands around her and had even unfastened her bra. His hands were just ready to cup her breasts.

"Cory," she screamed, "you can't do that." Her hand came up and slapped his face fairly hard. "What is wrong with you anyway?"

"Just in love, Sweetie, and trying to give you a little sample of what you're going to experience after you say I do," he chuckled as he rubbed his cheek. "You've got quite a wallop there, and I'm sorry, Sweetheart, I got carried away again. Sit up and turn around and I'll get you fastened back up. I'd never done that before and just wondered if I could actually do it." As she turned her back toward him, his one hand quickly went around and cupped her breast which caused another reaction that thrilled him. "Um, that's nice," he whispered as he caressed the nipple and was so softly kissing her neck and nibbling her earlobe. She hadn't said a word but he could feel her body movements. "Would you like for me to continue?" he softly whispered, but was chuckling as he fastened the bra. He just kissed her cheek and went on to the kitchen to make some coffee while she was pulling her sweater down and going to her bedroom to fix her hair and makeup although completely unsure of what had just happened. When she joined him in the kitchen, she looked a little embarrassed, so he decided she'd had enough surprises for one day. But then she very shyly asked, "Cory, are you really being honest with me? I really do enjoy learning some of these things, but are they what you should be doing right now?"

"Well, Sweetheart, being in love makes a guy want to do a lot of things, but I'll try to wait for our wedding night to show you what I think love really can be like—as if I'm an expert at all this," he chuckled. "Let's change the subject now and get to some things that will need our attention rather shortly." He started discussing his mother's call, and then they tried to figure out how they could learn not to step on each other's toes. He laughingly warned his tigress, "My mom wouldn't take kindly to me coming to her door seeking refuge each time you decide to lock me out of the house."

She immediately went to a drawer, pulled out a key, and placed it in his hand. "Now I can't lock you out anymore. I'll have to find another way to punish you when you're bad," she giggled as she gave him a quick kiss on his cheek.

Of course, Cory grabbed her and gave her a real romantic kiss before he'd let her go. "It's hard to keep my hands off you, you know. I just wish I'd met you sooner. I was a fool to decline the invitations your dad made to meet you, but it could be for the best. You may have turned me down flat back then and where would I be now?"

After they'd finished their coffee and a rather late lunch, they decided to take a walk which took them down by the cottage Marshall had bought, but they were surprised to see not only his car but also a pickup in the driveway. "What do you suppose he's doing?" she asked as they stood trying to see in the windows.

It's really none of our business, Andrea, since he has bought the place and can do anything he wants to it. We'd better continue our walk and refrain from being the old nosey neighbors before we scare him off and he escapes back to Boston. I definitely want him here in the office."

"Oh, look, Cory. There they are and they're looking at a paint brochure. I'll bet he's going to have some of the walls painted so it will be nice and clean when he has his things delivered. I didn't think men cared about such things. Mom and I were always the ones who took care of the decorating."

"Someone once said that you learn something new every day, and I guess it must be true. Shall we be on our way now and stop our snooping?" It was too late, though, because at that moment the door opened and Marshall stepped out onto the porch. "You could've just come to the door and knocked," he chuckled. "Come on in and give me your opinions on the colors of paint I should choose."

With Andrea's help, it didn't take Marshall long to make his decision and the painter was smiling as he left. "Thank you so much, Andrea, you've been a great help. I probably would've chosen a different color for every room and then hated it. I'm glad you guys were snoopy today because you just saved me the time and expense of another paint job."

"Why don't you come on down and take a look at the way Andrea has changed the appearance of each room by using different colors as accents?" Cory asked as they were all heading for the door. "It's definitely a woman's touch, I guess, and we men will just have to live with it," he grinned, wrapping his arm around her and kissing her on the forehead.

"I can't today, Guys, but thanks anyway. I have another appointment and then I may drive on to Boston tonight so I can go to church tomorrow and then do some more packing of the things I want to bring back with me. You'll probably have me on your doorstep a lot when I get moved in, but I sure thank both of you for making this weekend special. I'll see you when I get back."

"Remember you'll be driving on a Saturday night."

"Yes, Father," he chuckled as he got in his car and drove away."

## Chapter Fifteen

After attending the Worship Service Sunday morning, Cory and Andrea stopped at the cafe, got a sandwich and fries, and then decided to walk down and check the boat. The sun was shining so brightly that the cabin was quite warm from the rays coming through the windows. It was a beautiful interior with a beige upholstered couch and 2 chairs and cherry tables, cabinets, etc. They felt so comfy that they decided to stay awhile and discuss several things they needed to consider while enjoying a few more kisses and touches that she was finding quite exciting.

"About the car we both apparently want to give to Jason," Cory remarked. "After some time to think about it, are you really sure you want to let go of the Cherokee?"

"Yes, Cory, I would love to see Jason have my dad's car, and I think he would be very pleased, too, to have a young, responsible boy like Jason have good transportation to drive to work and then on to college."

"O.K., that's settled. Now, how do you really feel about my staying at the cottage with you after Mom and Sissy get here from Quincy? Is there another solution that might be better? I know I'm not supposed to see you on our wedding day, and it's going to be a little awkward with both of us in the same house."

"I've been giving some thought to that since your mother called yesterday and also called my attention to the fact that we aren't supposed to see each other until we get to the church. I was wondering how it would work out if Sissy were to stay with me and your mom would stay with you. It would give me a chance to get to know her, and maybe she could help with some of the cooking and other arrangements. Do you think they would agree to that? I know you only have a futon in the spare room so would that be comfortable enough for her?

"That sounds like an excellent plan, Sweetie. I'll sleep on the futon and Mom can have my bed. I'll call her tonight and see what she and Sissy think about it."

They then discussed their schedules for Monday and decided they would drive into Plymouth on Tuesday to see about her new car. Her face beamed as she anticipated finally buying the car she'd wanted for years. When they returned to the cottage, it was almost 5 o'clock. He remembered that he had some papers he needed to go over for an appointment early on Monday morning, so after a quick bowl of soup and a few long goodnight kisses, he left to tend to business.

Monday turned out to be an unusual day for Andrea. She didn't call ahead to see if Pastor Avery would be free to see her, so when she got there, of course he was in a meeting. The secretary had buzzed his office to tell him Andrea would like to see him, and he'd just replied, "Send her in, she might be of some help to us."

*Well, I have no idea what this is about, but I'm game to find out.* The Pastor opened the door and motioned for her to come in where she saw two other men and a woman. She recognized one of the men as Mr. Dean Capland of the Capland Builders, one of the largest contractors in the area and also a member of the church. She was introduced and learned that the other two, Susan Hepburn and Steve Maynor, were realtors in the County, and they were discussing the dire need for homes in the area and if the church could possibly help in some way.

"It seems that people want to live here, but we've had absolutely nothing to offer them for some time," Steve offered as an explanation. "One cottage was sold recently and that's it. It turns out that most inquiries are for either larger family homes or townhouses and places where yard care and maintenance would be taken care of under a contract with a home owners' association."

"Why can't we provide some of those?" Andrea asked. "I've seen a few of those gated townhouse communities which not only provide security for the part-time residents, but I've also loved the landscaping that can be done in those areas. I really fell in love with one that had a huge fountain right inside the gate that you could drive around to get to the office. It had a walking path around the perimeter with trees, shrubs, and flowers that gave a relaxing atmosphere, and also benches were supplied in areas along the path. At the opposite end from the entrance, there was a pool, tennis courts, and a play area. All the homes had nice private back yards with trees, hedges or shrubs maintained by the association, but it also left plenty of room for individual plantings."

She stopped and laughingly said, "I guess I'm really getting carried away, but I was wondering if that land on the edge of town would be suitable. I understand the executor is trying to sell so he can close the estate."

"I've inquired about it, inspected it, and determined that it would be a perfect location, Andrea, and I'd be willing to buy the land," Mr. Capland replied, "but we'll also need capital to get it surveyed, divided into lots, water, sewer, electric and phone lines installed, and also roads constructed. It would be a wonderful addition to our little town, bringing work and homes for those wanting to locate here. That, in turn, can always bring new business, more families, and ideas for growth and soon we'd have a thriving little community."

"Well, I don't know much about the building trade, but I'd be willing to provide, or at least help provide, funds to do the necessary groundwork you mentioned to get the project going—on one condition, of course," she grinned. "I've heard that Mr. Anderson, who was injured while working for you, wants to do some drawing, or whatever you call it, and some friends and family are providing him with a drafting table, a computer, and all the other items he needs for doing this at his home. I'll need his expertise before next Spring because I'm planning to enlarge my cottage, and I'll want to hire your crew, too. Would you be willing to ask Mr. Anderson to do the plans for this townhouse subdivision?"

"You bet, he was the best worker I ever had, and he drew some great blueprints for me, too. I'm thrilled to hear that he wants to get back to work. But are you sure you want to invest in this? I'm afraid it could be several million dollars to get the project off the ground. I don't know what your father's estate consisted of, but I want you to know up front what we're facing to just get the project started. Any amount you feel you could invest would certainly help and you would get a return on your money, of course, because all the expenses are totaled and included in the price of the units."

"That sounds like a good investment to me, so let me know when you have the figures drawn up and I'll agree to put a substantial amount in the project. But, I almost forgot that I have another condition," she giggled. "My future husband, Cory Calhoun, is the attorney here in town, and I'd like for him to handle all the legal matters."

Laughing and chuckling, they remarked "Who else?" as they unanimously agreed.

Then the Pastor turned to her and asked, "What was the reason for your visit today, Andrea? We've sort of monopolized your time. Can I, or can we, help *you* with something now?"

"Oh, yes, I wanted to find out if you know of a wedding coordinator that I could get in touch with. I've realized that I have no knowledge at all about planning a wedding, but even though mine is going to be rather small, I want it to be special."

With a big smile, the Pastor said, "I think we can help you with that, Andrea. With the real estate business a little slow the last few years, Susan here has stepped in and become our wedding coordinator. Our former one moved away, but Susan has done a fine job."

After he'd stood to shake hands with Dean and Steve as they were leaving, he glanced at his watch and turned to Andrea and Susan. "I have an errand to run, but if you both have time, you may stay right here to discuss your wedding plans unless you'd rather take her to your office down the hall, Susan." He then slipped out the door.

"I'd be more than happy to help you, Andrea, but it's up to you. I don't think he really meant to, but Pastor Avery was a little forward with the assumption that I was the one you needed."

"Oh, I didn't take it that way at all. Ah,—may I call you Susan? I'd love to have you help me so I don't make a complete mess of my wedding. I have a few things I've always wanted included in my wedding, but I don't know the first thing about getting it done."

"Let's go to my office, then, so I have my pad to take notes, and I can also show you a few ideas on how the sanctuary can be set up. Did you say it will be a small wedding? If it's going to be for 25 or less guests, maybe you'd like to take a look at the chapel instead of the large sanctuary. It's a wonderfully warm and congenial setting for a small wedding."

"As far as I know right now," Andrea laughed, "it will be far below 25, but the way my fiance' keeps inviting all his clients, I'm not sure how many will end up being here, but the chapel sounds intriguing. Since my dad passed away, I won't have anyone to give me away, so I don't need an aisle to walk down."

"Oh, you'll have an aisle, Andrea, just not quite as long as in the sanctuary. Let's go and have a look at the chapel and its possibilities before we start putting anything down in writing."

The chapel was absolutely beautiful with three large stained glass windows forming a wrap around for the altar, plus ample room for candelabra, the unity candle, and flowers. The lighting was soft and soothing and the padded pews would easily seat 25, as Susan had said, if not a few more. There was a small organ and a nice upholstered chair for the soloist down by the first pew. Andrea was positive this was where she wanted to be married, so they went to Susan's office to make the other decisions.

Andrea was so excited when she left the church that she just had to share it with some one. *I don't know her too well, but she is coming to my home for Thanksgiving dinner, and she is going to be my attendant, so I think she would be very interested in my decisions.* She used her cell phone to call Grace, but of course, Roger answered. "Well, hello Clayton, have you made plans for tearing the cottage or boat apart yet?" She quickly realized it definitely had sounded a little too sarcastic but could only shudder as Roger replied.

"Hello to you, too, Andrea Harrington. I thought we'd gotten past that episode in our lives. I guess your dad didn't realize you'd carry a grudge after his scheme worked and you'd fallen in love with Cory. What can I do for you today?"

"I'm sorry, Roger. I was just kidding, but I realize it didn't sound very nice. Will you forgive me? I'd like to talk to Grace, if she's up to it. I just met with a wedding coordinator and I am so excited, I really need to share with someone. How is she feeling, anyway? Oh, you don't know girl-talk. Is she napping or may I talk to her?"

"Hold on, Tiger, I'll get her. We just got back from Boston so she's right here."

*I wonder how much Cory has shared with him about my bad reactions to things, but he was the one who told Cory that I was an untamed tiger way back as a teenager. I guess my reputation has followed me for a long time, but I'm going to change. I have to if I'm going to be a good mother.*

"Hello, Andrea, I understand you have exciting news to share with me. Would you like to come up here? I'll send Roger some-place to do some-thing so we can talk all by ourselves," she giggled.

"Are you sure you're up to it after your trip? I thought you may have gotten back yesterday."

"I'm fine, really. That's my opinion as well as that of my gynecologist."

"I'm on my way, then. See you soon."

When she arrived, Roger was being pushed out the door. He had a slight smile on his face but he rather sarcastically commented, "I think you've had a bad influence on my wife, Andrea. I should've never told her about being thrown out of your house." Luckily, he did pat her cheek as he passed by and then turned to blow a kiss to Grace before he strolled off down the hill.

The two girls had a great time talking about the wedding plans, and decided they'd better drive to Plymouth one day soon to find their dresses although there was a little shop right here in town that they could visit. It was a little past noon when Andrea was getting ready to leave, but in walked Roger with Cory tagging behind. A sack of sandwiches from the cafe was in Roger's hand so they enjoyed the lunch together as they discussed using the chapel for the wedding and then talked about Grace and the baby. She'd been declared fit as a fiddle by her doctor and is feeling great except for having some morning sickness still giving her discomfort a few hours each day.

Andrea gave Cory a ride back to his office, kissed him goodbye and headed home, her mind chocked full of wedding plans.

# *Chapter Sixteen*

Cory and Andrea planned to leave early Tuesday morning to drive to Plymouth to get the new car she'd really been dreaming about ever since they'd been debating the idea of giving her dad's car to Jason. Cory had finally agreed that her suggestion of the Cherokee would be a good solution, so they are now going to buy the car of her dreams. Cory had arrived at the cottage at 8:30, but just as they reached the edge of town, they saw the flashing lights of a police car just ahead. It appeared to be in front of the Hobby and Crafts Store, and suddenly Cory's heart was in his throat as he quietly remarked, "Oh, no, it's Jason's car up against the parking lot light pole. Please, Dear God, don't let Jason be hurt badly."

Cory turned into the parking lot and noticed another car just in front of him, without a driver, facing out the Entrance driveway. Several people had gathered but as he scanned the area, he saw Jason standing with Police Chief Winters and another man. When he'd parked his car, he approached the three.

When Jason saw him, he looked concerned as he said, "Hi, Mr. Calhoun, I'd like you to meet Police Chief Winters, and also Mr. Larry Green who owns the car over there that I hit when my brakes failed. He turned to the others and said, "This is my very good friend, Cory Calhoun, our attorney in town. If you ever need an attorney, he's great."

Extending his hand to the Chief, Cory remarked smiling, "I have met the Chief, but it is good to see you again, Sir, and it's nice to meet you, Mr. Green," as he also shook his hand. "Jason likes to exaggerate a little at times, but I do my best to solve problems. So, do we have a problem here that I may be able to help with?"

"The only problem that I see, Mr. Calhoun, is that Jason is without a car," the Chief replied. "Mr. Green says that it did nothing except put a small nick in his back bumper that caused him to spin around so he's heading out the wrong driveway. He doesn't intend to ask for any payment or to press charges. Jason's car, however, has no brakes and apparently got a rather hard rap to the front end, when it hit the pole, because the radiator is now leaking. We'll have to have the wrecker come and tow it, I'm afraid. Of course, we're just glad he had his seat belt fastened so he wasn't thrown into the wheel or the windshield."

"Yes, thank God for that. I think Andrea Harrington and I can solve the problem of him being without a car, and I'll pay for this car to be towed to the junk yard, if that's okay with Jason. Turning to his troubled young friend, he asked, "Do you have any papers or personal items you need to get out of it first?"

"The insurance certificate is in the glove compartment, and I have another jacket and some tools in the trunk, but, Mr. Calhoun, I don't have the money for another car. I could only afford liability insurance, but couldn't I try to get this one fixed?"

"No, Jason, brakes are not an inexpensive thing to have fixed, let alone a new radiator and who knows what else. And even if you did that, you'd still have an old car that isn't safe for you to drive, especially when you get ready to go to college."

Turning to the Chief, he said, "If we can take Jason for a few minutes, we'll see that he has a car to drive that's insured for him to drive with our permission. Later, we'll see that everything is put in order. I've promised to take Andrea into Plymouth today so she can make an important purchase or I'd take care of everything right now. One other thing, however, do you think Jason should be checked by a doctor?"

"One of the doctors from the Clinic just happened to be going by and so he stopped to see if he might be needed. He checked Jason and said he seemed fine, but if he started to feel any pain or dizziness, he should have someone bring him to the Clinic."

Jason could do nothing but stare at this man who had already saved him from going to prison, kept his name out of the news, and now is saying he has a car for him, not to mention what he was doing for his dad. He felt as if he were in a dream, but about that time another man approached and Jason introduced him as the manager of the Hobby and Crafts Store. He had been on the scene before so he knew the circumstances and readily agreed that Jason was to come to work, if he felt up to it, after arrangements had been made for him to have some transportation.

The Chief said he would see that a tow truck was called, so after Jason had retrieved his belongings, he joined Cory and Andrea and they returned to the cottage. Andrea went inside to get the keys to the Cherokee, and when she came back and handed them to Jason, she also gave him a hug, which embarrassed him, of course. She then told him that her dad would be so proud to know that such a nice young man was now driving his car.

Cory showed him a few things he thought might be different from driving his old car, and they waited for him to back out of the drive and head back to work. Cory and Andrea looked at each other and smiled. "He is such a deserving kid," Cory remarked as he pulled her into his arms and hugged her tight. "Shall we be on our way, Sweetie?"

It was a beautiful day, and Andrea was so happy when she found the car right away that made her heart beat just like she remembered it did when she was little and she'd gotten the doll she'd wanted so desperately for Christmas.

After they'd eaten lunch, Cory spotted a Men's Formal Wear Shoppe and decided he should buy his tux for the wedding while they were right here. Roger had told him that he owned one so he didn't have to worry about him.

Andrea insisted that he try two or three different styles before she decided which one she liked the best. The clerk was very patient, Cory thought, since he knew he would've just taken the first one he'd tried on and that would've been that, but he'd made the mistake of doing it when Andrea was along. He had to admit, however with a chuckle, that the one she finally picked was an exceptional tuxedo even though it was the first one he'd tried on.

When they got back outdoors, he noticed that she was looking around at the shops nearby so he asked, although he knew the answer, if she wanted him to help her select her wedding dress. She replied, "That'll be the day, Mr. Calhoun," and headed for his car. "It's about the time they said we could pick up my car, so should we head back there? I'd like to get home before the 5 o'clock traffic starts on the highway."

"Are you going to protect this car like you would a child?" he asked as they were driving toward the dealership. "It's just a commodity, you know, and I hope you don't ever consider it more precious than your friends, your family, or your faith in God." He looked at her with concern in his eyes as she had been so excited about this particular car.

"Of course not," she glared at him. "I'm excited about owning a car I've admired for quite awhile, but I won't ever put it before God or you or my future family. I'm sorry if I've given that impression, Cory, because the friends I've made recently could never be replaced with a piece of steel or whatever cars are made of anymore. I loved the look in Jason's eyes when I handed him the keys to the Cherokee, and I just realized how much more that meant to me than it will to receive the keys to this new one. I think I would have been just as happy if I'd bought any other elegant looking sedan. I just didn't like the Cherokee and I think that was because I'd always associated that type of car with Dad or a male driver."

"I'm glad we had this little talk, Andrea, and I'll never doubt your intentions again. I do want you to have the things you like, but I'm so glad you feel that God's creations are more important than things."

"Cory," she said quietly, "there's something else I promised to do when I saw the Pastor yesterday. I hope you won't be too upset with me, but I felt compelled to help when I heard about the dire need of homes in the area. Mr. Capland, the contractor, and two realtors were with Pastor Avery when I got there and he invited me to join them. There was some talk about that piece of land right at the edge of town that I think is involved in that estate you're handling. Well, Mr. Capland has checked it all out and is willing to buy the land, but he doesn't have the capital to do all the other preliminary work before the actual building can begin. He promises I'll get a good return on my money, so I agreed to provide at least a portion of what's needed for the surveying, utilities, and roads." She waited for his reaction to this latest wild involvement of hers, but he was very quiet as if in deep thought.

They had pulled into the dealership before he spoke, "Mr. Capland has talked to me about that land and I knew he had looked at it; but Andrea, I really wish you had spoken to me first before you promised to do something like that, because," he hesitated as he tried to portray a disappointment, "Sweetie, I would've loved to have been your partner in such an investment." He was now grinning as he pulled her over to give her a quick kiss and then started to open his door to come around and open the door for her.

"Wait a minute, Cory, before you get out. They probably won't need the money until after we're married, maybe not until Spring, so why couldn't we be partners? I told them I'd do it under two conditions—one that Mr. Anderson would be hired as the architect, and the other that you would be the attorney for all the legal matters." Smiling, she watched as he, with the biggest grin on his face, again opened his door and scooted around to get her.

He was so proud of his bride-to-be, his heart was overflowing. "You are absolutely the greatest, do you know that?" he asked as he pulled her into his arms and kissed her right there at the busy car dealership.

The car was ready to go, so with Andrea in the lead and Cory following, they drove out of Plymouth and headed toward home with their thoughts on the future when they could definitely do things as a team.

Cory had told Andrea that he wanted to stop at the office when they got back in town, and he'd come over after putting his magnificent new tux in a safe place. He had to smile as he remembered the endearing wifely way she'd checked every detail of each tux she'd asked him to model before they'd settled on the first one.

It was about 4:30 when he entered the office and found Donna ready to close. She was on her way to his office with messages when she heard the door open and turned to greet him with her usual smile. "Glad you're back safely, Boss, it has been quite lonely here all by myself, but there were a couple of distractions," she grinned. "Bryan Munson, the young man whose wife wanted a divorce, called to let you know that she has changed her mind after moving back into her parents' home. She'd quickly realized how difficult it was with their attitude toward her; being away for almost four years, some at college and some in the marriage; and how much she missed him day after day. She's apparently willing to go to counseling now, so he said he'd drop in to see you soon.

The other," she continued, "was a visit from Jason after he got off work at 3 o'clock. He said he'd worked later to make up for the time he'd missed this morning. He wanted to thank you again and try to make some kind of arrangements to pay you for all you've done. Did something else happen, Cory? It looked to me like he was driving Mr. Harrington's, or I should say Andrea's, Cherokee. Am I right?"

Smiling, he said, "You're right, Donna," and then proceeded to tell her about the early morning accident as he and Andrea were heading out of town. "We'll get the title and other papers transferred tomorrow and also get insurance in Jason's name."

"That'll cost a pretty penny with him only 18 or 19 years old."

"Yes, Donna, it will cost some money, but what good is money if you can't help some very deserving young person with it? I certainly received help when my pockets were rather empty. By the way, let me tell you what my incredible wife-to-be did yesterday to help our little town. A new subdivision is going to be started as soon as possible which will most likely include the sale of the acreage in that estate we're trying to close. Andrea's promised to supply capital for all or part of the preparatory requirements which will really start the ball rolling, and she's even willing to let my name be included because we'll be married before all the plans are worked out and they need the money. Isn't she just the greatest?"

"You two are such wonderful residents of this little town, and I'm so happy, Cory, that you asked me to come here with you so I can be a part of it, too."

"Thanks, Donna, but I'm so fortunate that you were willing to come, and you've been a life saver for me through some of those difficult and doubting times. However, this is going to give you a lot more work because Andrea has promised the money on two special conditions—that Mr. Anderson be the architect on the project, and that we'll do all the legal work."

"Oh, Cory, that's sensational! I'm going home now and dream of the busy days that are ahead of us. Do I get a raise when all the money comes pouring in?" she laughed as she headed toward the door. "God must've known all this was going to happen. That's why he sent Marshall our way just when He did. Goodnight, Boss."

Cory sat at his desk and marveled at all the things that had happened in just the last few months, and then he bowed his head and started to pray. He was suddenly aware of a loud tapping at the door and hurried to see who would be coming by at this hour. He was really surprised to see the Chief of Police standing there with a big smile on his face. He quickly unlocked the door, opened it and asked Chief Winters to come in. "Did everything go all right this morning after we left?" he asked.

"Mr. Calhoun, I can't begin to describe what has happened today in this little town. It was like a miracle had happened in that boy's life when he pulled into the parking lot in that Grand Cherokee, and you should've seen the look on his face when I presented him the money we had gotten from that wreck of a car. I don't know what your plans are—I wish I could help him own that car—but, of course that's impossible in my job. I just came by to thank you for what you did this morning. It was definitely a miracle in my eyes."

"Thanks, Chief, but it was just the conclusion of something Andrea and I had wanted to do but hadn't decided when to do it. The car is his, free and clear, and we'll get the title and all that stuff transferred tomorrow. We'll also plan to see that the insurance is maintained on it until he is out of college, has a job, and can handle that by himself."

"Well, Jason and the car isn't the only thing I heard about today. I also learned there is going to be a new subdivision developed and that Andrea, at least, is involved in that plan. I got to know her father quite well, and I could imagine him doing something like this, but I've never gotten to know Andrea very well, because of her being away in college and then working in New York, so I didn't know how she might regard her father's adopted home."

"As far as our plans are right now, we're both here to stay. We're getting married on the Saturday right after Thanksgiving, at 3 o'clock. Andrea is already talking about how to enlarge the cottage so we can have more than one child, and I'm adding another attorney in my practice so we'll be set to handle all the extra work this subdivision will provide.

You're very welcome to come to the wedding, Chief. It's going to be a very small affair, so the more the merrier if you'd like to come. I'm sorry, I don't know if you have a wife or not, but you're certainly welcome to bring someone with you.

"My wife heard about the wedding from one of her friends," he said, grinning. "As you know, nothing remains a secret very long in this town, and I imagine she would love to attend since she knew Andrea when she and our daughter ran around together. I'll tell her we're invited and maybe she'll see if Tammy would like to stay over the weekend, when she and her husband come for Thanksgiving. I'll probably be on duty, and her husband is usually anxious to get back to his shop, but they could drive both cars or he could come back to get her on Sunday. They just live about 15 minutes away. Thanks, Mr. Calhoun, but I'd better get back to the office now."

"You're very welcome, Chief, and I'd like it if you would call me Cory. In this little town, we shouldn't have to be so formal, should we?" he chuckled.

"I appreciate that, Cory. Goodbye, now."

Time had certainly slipped by, and it was really dark when Cory reached the cottage, so he was surprised that there were no lights on inside. *What in the world is that girl doing in there without lights,* he wondered as he turned into the drive, but then he saw that the lights were on in the garage and let out a groan. *She has fallen in love with that car and is going to live in it,* he grumbled to himself as he pulled his car almost to the garage door before getting out. Slipping into the garage through the side door, he saw her sitting in the front seat, with the manual in her hands, and so absorbed she wasn't hearing a thing. He couldn't help but smile. Not wanting to frighten her by appearing at the window, he gently tapped on the trunk and then peeked in her window.

She jumped but then giggled as she glanced at her watch. "Are you just getting here?" she asked as she opened the door. "I was just going to check a few things until you came, but I've read almost half the manual. What have you been doing?"

"It's been very interesting. Let's go in the house and I'll tell you about it, but maybe we should go get something to eat. Shall we try the restaurant that has the catering service as well as the restaurant? What's the name—Cathy's Bistro and Catering?"

"Oh, yes, I want to see that place and try their food. Susan is going to take me there tomorrow so I can see the private room they have for receptions and other parties. She says she has a wonderful idea on how to handle any number of guests that show up instead of having a specified number for a sit-down dinner. I understand they have a dance floor area, too."

"That sounds like an exceptionally good plan," he laughed as he took her in his arms and held her arms tight to her sides as he continued, "because there may be at least two more coming to our wedding."

She squirmed in his arms, but he held firm. "Who in the world have you found to invite now, you, you character!" she yelled as she threatened to bite his arm. He quickly dropped his hold and jumped away when he realized what she was thinking of doing.

"Andrea, you have to calm down because I can't go to our wedding with bruises on my arms from you hitting or biting me," he laughed. "Somebody might think you're going to be an abusing wife and call the police. That wouldn't look good when the Chief, or at least his wife and daughter, might be at the wedding. Do you remember a Tammy Winters who was your friend here in town? You didn't bite her, did you, so she won't want to see you get married?"

"I wasn't really going to bite you, Cory, but Tammy's dad is the Chief of Police? How did you happen to invite him or them? I was at their house a lot, but I don't remember ever meeting her dad. Maybe that's why—he was probably at the station or on patrol. She doesn't live here, does she?"

"No, she doesn't live here, but she and her husband live about 15 minutes away and they are planning to be here for Thanksgiving. The Chief thinks he'll probably be on duty, but his wife and Tammy might like to come. Her husband, apparently, has a shop that he likes to get back to, but Tammy could stay for the weekend."

"Oh, that's so exciting, Cory. I apologize for getting upset and I'll forgive you once again for adding to those attending our wedding. You'd better slow down, though, or we'll have to use the sanctuary, and I've fallen in love with that cozy little chapel."

"I'll try not to invite anyone else, although," he hesitated, wondering if it would help the cause if he invited two more.

"Although, what, Mr. Calhoun. What is going on in that head of yours now?"

"Do you remember the young man, Bryan Munson, whose wife had wanted a divorce and I suggested that he might talk to you? Well, he called today and told Donna that his wife has changed her mind, since going to her parents' home and realizing how difficult that was and how much she missed him. He said he'd drop by to see me soon, and I was just thinking that if they attended a wedding, it might help their situation. You know, maybe put them in that lovey-dovey mood, so to speak," he grinned and fluttered those sexy eyelashes.

"If I agree to those two, will you promise to stop asking?"

"The time is getting short, isn't it, and you have to know the number coming so you can finalize your plans for the reception and make sure they'll all fit in the chapel. Okay, Sweetheart, I won't ask another soul."

"Fine, let's go to Cathy's Bistro and get something to eat now so I can taste what their food is like and then decide if that is where I want our reception."

# *Chapter Seventeen*

Andrea was so excited when Susan picked her up Wednesday morning. They were to see the room at Cathy's Bistro & Catering and make arrangements for the reception. She and Cory had enjoyed their meal there last night and was also very impressed with the decor of the restaurant, so she's anxious now to see the room where special events are held.

Cathy turned out to be a wonderful hostess and guide, and when she and Susan had finished explaining the plans for setting up the room, Andrea was elated. The dance floor is in the far corner, and different sized tables will be arranged around the curved edge. The cake, which Andrea selected from samples in a booklet, along with mints and nuts, will be on the center table of a 3-piece arrangement in the corner to the right of the dance floor, and it will have rollers so it can easily be moved to the center of the dance floor when the bride and groom cut their traditional piece of cake. It will then roll back between the other two tables which will hold the punch and coffee.

The other two corners will hold all kinds of food from shrimp, buffalo wings, chicken tenders, sandwich fixings, chips, potato salad, a vegetable salad, different cheeses, fruit and relish trays, and drinks to be enjoyed throughout the evening. A three or four-piece ensemble will be playing for an hour or more before a break is called for the bride and groom to cut the cake and for the people to be served. It will then resume playing for more dancing, listening, and chatting.

When they'd finished at Cathy's, they went to the flower shop to pick the flowers for the chapel and make tentative plans for the bouquets, the mother and sister corsages, and the boutonnieres. Susan asked about an usher, and when Andrea thought that maybe Marshall would do that, they added another boutonniere. They then stopped for a quick lunch before Susan dropped her off at the cottage. Andrea was almost in tears because she was so happy. She knew her wedding was going to be exactly what she had always dreamed it would be.

As she headed for her door, Andrea just happened to glance toward the cottage that Marshall had bought. She saw that the painter's truck was there as it had been Monday and Tuesday. She wondered how he was getting along, but she didn't linger.

*I'm sort of glad that I don't have to worry about his cottage as I need to call Grace and see when we can go to look for our dresses and the other feminine items I need to buy.* She giggled as she thought of the almost worn out gowns she'd been wearing and ones Cory had caught her in at least twice. When they talked, she and Grace decided to try the little bridal shop in town on Friday. It had opened about a year ago, but neither of them had been inside. If they couldn't find what they wanted here in town, then they would go to Plymouth next week.

On Thursday, Andrea decided to go for a bicycle ride, something she had neglected lately except for the one time she and Cory had stretched their muscles riding out into the country. When she went by Marshall's cottage, about 1 o'clock, the painter was getting into his truck. He smiled and waved as he told her he had just finished the painting.

On her way back, however, there was another car, in about the same shape as Cory had described Jason's, parked in the driveway. She could see that someone was moving around inside and decided she'd better make sure everything was alright. Perhaps the painter had left the door unlocked and someone was in there snooping around or planning to do some vandalism. She had just reached the door when it started to open, so she quickly flattened herself against the wall of the house and watched as a woman and a child appeared. They'd actually startled each other, and then Andrea giggled as she recognized her. "Oh, I'm sorry, Mrs. Anderson, I was just wondering who would be in the house since I saw the painter leave earlier this afternoon. Did Marshall ask you to clean after the painting was finished?"

"Yes, he contacted me last Saturday, before he returned to Boston, and said he'd have the painter inform me when he was finished. Is there a problem, Andrea? Oh," she smiled, "Mr. Walker did say not to worry if a couple of friends came by acting a little too nosey. You wouldn't be one of those he was referring to, now, would you?"

"I guess I was being rather snoopy," she snickered, "but I was concerned that there might possibly be someone snooping around and would maybe do some vandalism. Is this Janie? I haven't seen her for so long. I think she was still a baby when I went off to college."

"Yes, this is our Janie, and she's eight now. She had the sniffles today so I kept her home from school. Mr. Capland called wanting to come and talk to her daddy, and I had to bring her along with me. I was just going to the car for some of my supplies. Did you want to look inside? The walls and ceilings look great. I hope I can get the cabinets cleaned as well as the floors, woodwork, and windows before he returns."

Just then Janie spoke up, "Jason and Sam are invited to your wedding, aren't they? I wish I could go to a wedding—they are so pretty. I was just five years old when my big sister got married, so I don't remember it too well."

"Well, Janie, I see no reason why you couldn't come with your brothers to Cory and my wedding. Your mom and dad are welcome to come, too, if they'd like. The ceremony is going to be at 3 o'clock in the Chapel of our church, and the reception will be in the banquet room at Cathy's Bistro. We'd love to have you come and there will be plenty of room for the wheelchair at both places."

"Andrea, do you really mean that? I'm sorry that Janie talked out of turn, but Jason and Sam are so excited that it has rubbed off on the rest of us, I guess. Mr. Calhoun has made such an impression on our boys, and they think the world of him. Jason just couldn't believe it when he invited him and

Sam to the wedding, much less all the other things the two of you have done for our family."

"Please don't worry about what Janie said, Mrs. Anderson, and we'll be thrilled to have all of you attend the wedding and reception. Mr. Anderson could sit in his wheelchair in the chapel, if he'd like, because there's that space at the back of the room, and a few extra chairs could be added in case you'd like to sit with him. We'll have a table at the reception to accommodate your family. I do hope you'll plan to come, but I'd better let you get back to your work. I'm so glad I got to speak to you. As far as those other things, helping others is just one of the traits my dad saw in Cory when he chose him for his attorney and, actually, he picked him for my husband, too," she giggled.

Andrea was singing as she pedaled on home. She realized it was a good time to get her mother's beautiful Thanksgiving items out and decorate the cottage. It included an over—flowing cornucopia as the centerpiece on the table, an early American village on the mantel, and all kinds of ceramic Pilgrims, Indians, and pumpkins placed here and there. Of course, there had to be an abundance of candles like she and her mother had always loved to have burning on all the holidays. She had cleaned as she put things in their places and was pleased with the look when she'd finished. She was concentrating so hard on her task that she was startled when the phone started ringing.

"Hey, it's Andrea," she answered, thinking it would be Cory, but was disappointed when it was another telemarketer trying to sell her something. When she glanced at her watch, however, she saw that it was almost 6:30, and she was surprised that Cory hadn't come by, or at least called. Could there have been a late client? She really didn't want to interrupt a meeting, if that was the case, so she decided to call his apartment and see if she might find him there. They hadn't made any plans for tonight, but he usually called anyway so she wanted to make sure he was all right. After dialing and listening to several rings, she was about ready to hang up. *Where could he be? Maybe Roger came to talk to him about some details of the wedding or some other plan they're working on.*

And then she heard a voice struggling to say, "Hell-o, this—is—Cory." But it didn't sound like Cory—it sounded like someone who had just been awakened out of a deep sleep and was finding it hard to speak.

"Cory, this is Andrea. Are you all right, Honey? Your voice sounds like you've been sleeping or that you're sick. Oh, Cory, are you sick? Can I come over and take care of you?"

She heard a little chuckle, which confused her, but then she heard him speak and knew that his voice was not normal.

"Andrea, Darling," he rasped, "as much as I'd love to see you, I really don't feel up to it tonight. My head is hurting and I think I've lost everything that was in my stomach. I don't know if it's just a headache, a touch of the flu, or something I ate for lunch, but Donna urged me to come home about 3 o'clock. After vomiting several times, I've been sleeping now, I see, for almost three hours. I think I need to get back to bed now. Oh, my head is whirling, Sweetie, so I'll talk to you tomorrow." She heard him place the phone in the cradle.

*You're out of your mind, Cory Calhoun, if you think I'm going to let you lie there all by yourself when we don't know what caused this upset. I'm going to call the doctor and then I'm going to see that you're taken care of.*

She learned from Dr. Haskell that a-24 hour flu was going around and several calls had come in to his office just this afternoon. Cory most likely needed some medication and also a lot of liquids to keep him from getting dehydrated. He told her he'd meet her at Cory's apartment in 30 minutes, which would give her time to get some tea, ginger ale, and crackers for him.

When they arrived at the apartment, they found Cory on the floor of his bedroom where he had slumped, apparently, after they'd talked. With both of them helping, they got him into his bed and gave him some medication. He had a temperature, so Andrea started applying a cool cloth to his face and got him to drink some tea. She saw a smile on his face as he murmured, "Thank you, Sweetheart," and then he drifted off to sleep.

"Can you stay here with him, Andrea, or should I have him transported to the hospital in Plymouth? We have several cases already at the clinic and the hospital is also filling up, so I'd rather he stay right here, but not unless he has someone to watch him."

"I won't be leaving, Doctor Haskell, and I'll call you if I think he's getting any worse. I'll see that he takes his medicine and drinks plenty of liquids. Is there anything else I should watch for?"

"He may be chilling so make sure he has plenty of covers, especially if you see that he is shivering. I'll come by in the morning on my way to the office."

Andrea sat by his bed for hours applying the cool cloth, making him take the pills and drink some more tea. When he seemed to be resting a little easier, she pulled a bigger and more comfortable chair from the living room, found a blanket, and also fell asleep. She woke the next morning to find Cory lying on his side watching her. "Now I really want to marry you, Sweetie, because I know you'll take care of me if I'm well or sick."

"You didn't know that before?" she asked. "I must appear terribly egotistical and self-centered if you think I would ever let you be by yourself when you're sick."

"I didn't mean it that way, Sweetie. I guess I'm not thinking too clearly yet this morning. My head feels like it has the drummer boy playing in it, but my stomach feels a lot better. Maybe I could try some of those crackers and some more tea if you feel like getting them for me."

"Of course," but as she headed for the kitchen, the doorbell rang. The doctor had come by to see how things were going, and he visited with Cory while Andrea fixed the tea and the crackers.

"I suggest you stay in bed most of the day, Cory, and you should be pretty much back to normal again by tonight. The more rest you get, the quicker you'll gain your full strength back. With a wedding coming up, you don't want to be under the weather," he chuckled. "By the way, did you get a flu shot this Fall? If not, I'd recommend you drop by the Clinic and get one so you don't have a repeat of this. If you need anything more, let me know. Now, I'd better be on my way to check on the rest of my patients."

❧

Andrea called Grace to tell her that their shopping trip would have to be postponed until next week, and then she found a book to read since Cory was sleeping again. It wasn't long until she realized her eyes were closing and she also slept.

It was almost noon when she was awakened by a kiss on her forehead, and she realized she was lying on the bed next to him. "When did you carry me to this bed, Cory Calhoun? You know you're sick and should not be doing such things," she scolded.

"You looked so uncomfortable when I had to get up around 10:30 and I couldn't let you continue to sleep in that chair. You don't weigh enough to hurt a flea, so don't get your feathers all in an uproar."

"I'll get ruffled feathers whenever I want, Cory, and you'd better learn to listen."

"I hear you, Sweetie, but are you getting hungry, by any chance?"

"I do believe I am," she answered still sounding a little perturbed as she sat up on the side of the bed. "What do you have that you feel you could eat, or should I go to the store or cafe?"

"I think I have some soups, maybe that chunkier Chicken & Noodles brand, but I think I should stick with some more crackers along with it. Did I hear you mention to the doctor that you'd brought some ginger ale? That sounds pretty good, too."

"Coming up, Master," she smirked as she headed for the kitchen.

Cory followed her to the kitchen but sat and waited at the table until she brought the soup, crackers and some cheese she'd found in the fridge. When finished with that, they took a glass of ginger ale and settled down on the couch to watch some TV until he decided they needed some more sleep. She was surprised to find that she was ready to stretch out again, too, and they were both sleeping soundly for the next three hours.

# Chapter Eighteen

It was after 4 o'clock when they were awakened by the doorbell ringing and then some soft knocking. Cory was up and grabbing his robe before Andrea was fully awake. When he glanced at his watch, he expected it to be Donna coming to check on him before going home. To his surprise, it was not only Donna, with a casserole in her hands, but Marshall was also standing there. "Hi, Guys, come on in. I'm almost normal again."

"I can't remember you ever being sick in Boston, Cory, so what's with this slacking off your office duties?" Marshall laughed accusingly.

Just then Andrea came into the room. Looking at her rumpled clothes and messy hair, Marshall really started chuckling. "Well, Andrea, were you possibly the cause of Cory being sick? Maybe this was all a planned pretend illness in order to spend some time with each other. What do you think, Donna?"

"No, I'll vouch for it being real, Marshall. No one could've faked the symptoms he had or the color of his skin. It was scary because I had never seen him sick before, either."

Just then there was a knock on the door. Since Marshall was the closest, he opened it and saw the doctor standing there. "Hello, Sir, with that little black bag. I'll assume you are a doctor coming to check on your patient. Come on in," he chuckled, "I'm Marshall Walker, an old friend of Cory's and actually a new attorney in his law office." He extended his hand and continued, "I just returned this afternoon to find him sort of neglecting his office duties so I guess I was doing a little teasing."

"You might as well get used to him, Dr. Haskell, because I'm hoping he's going to be around here for awhile. I couldn't have found a better friend or attorney to be in the office with me," Cory remarked.

"I'm Dr. Haskell and it's nice to meet you, Marshall. I think you'll be a somewhat jolly addition to our little town. I extend a hearty welcome." Turning back to Cory, he said, "You're looking much better than you did last night and this morning, and I hope you've thanked Andrea for calling me and staying with you last night. It smells like someone has been cooking. Do you feel like eating tonight, and what have you had so far today?"

"Andrea fixed me soup and some cheese and crackers, along with some ginger ale, a little before noon, but I'll admit I've been sleeping most of the day. I do feel like I can eat now, though, and Donna brought the casserole that smells delicious."

"I'll be on my way, then. Some of my patients aren't recovering quite so fast, and that's why I thought I'd drop by to see how you're doing. You must have had good TLC from Andrea. She was quite concerned. Don't forget that flu shot, Cory. Goodnight, Everyone."

"See, you must've had good TLC from Andrea—even the doctor noticed." Marshall was chuckling, but when he saw the look on Cory's face, he quickly added, "Sorry, I was just kidding. I'm sure Andrea has been here doing nursing duties and had to catch a few winks whenever she could."

"That is so true, Marsh. She's been a Florence Nightingale. She called the doctor in the first place, and then they came and found me on the floor of the bedroom where I'd slumped after talking to her on the phone. It took both of them to get me back into bed. She stayed up for hours in a chair by the bed before getting a little sleep."

"Gosh, Cory, did the doctor think it was the flu or maybe food poisoning?"

"He said the flu is going around. The medication helped so I assume that's what it was. I'd forgotten to get the flu shot this year. So, you're back a day early. Did you bring a lot of stuff with you?"

"I have my van full and was hoping for some help, but I see it's not going to come from you."

"No, I'm sorry about that, but I can get you some help. Do you need one, two or three sets of muscles?"

"Two would be great for carrying my bed frame and mattress in. I thought I'd try to bring one of the twin beds so I wouldn't have to sleep on the floor until the moving van arrives. One of my good neighbors helped me load it, and I was so lucky that it just fit in the van. By the way, I stopped at the cottage before coming over to the office, and I found Mrs. Anderson just finishing the cleaning. She did a fabulous job and everything is just sparkling, but have you seen the car she drives?"

"I have," Andrea spoke up as she came from the kitchen with a cup of tea for Cory. "I don't know how she makes it from one job to the next. Could I get anyone else a cup of tea or a soft drink?"

"I'd really love some tea, but I can fix it. You don't need to wait on me, Andrea," Donna insisted as she headed for the kitchen. "Marshall, can I bring you something?" she called as she was filling the teapot.

"Maybe a glass of water, Donna, if you don't mind."

Andrea spoke again, "If you guys could stay for just a little while, I'd love to run home and clean up. I've never worn the same outfit for two days and a night before in my life. I know how the homeless must feel now," she giggled.

"Run along, My Dear," Marshall chuckled, "I'll be happy to stay with my buddy here even if Donna wants to go home, but I think that casserole she brought will feed all of us. If it's all right with everyone else, I'm inviting myself and we'll eat as soon as you get back, and then I'll get the van unloaded."

"Maybe we should've sent him back to Boston," Donna laughed as she returned from the kitchen with her tea and a glass of ice water for Marshall.

Andrea was back in 45 minutes, freshly showered and in clean clothes. Cory had also showered and dressed. Andrea brought ingredients for a salad, and Donna had put the large casserole in the oven to re-warm. When the table was set, the four sat down to enjoy the meal together. It tasted so good to both Cory and Andrea after the soup, crackers, and tea diet they'd endured for over 24 hours.

"As I mentioned earlier," Marshall remarked during the meal, "I was shocked to see the car Mrs. Anderson has to drive, and then I heard the engine as she drove away. I was wondering if she would accept a car if it was offered. I want to keep my van, of course, but I also have the Honda Civic that I drove up here last week. It was Jaylene's and I haven't tried to sell it yet. It's five years old, but it only has about 25,000 miles on it. I certainly don't need two cars in this little town."

"It'll take a little doing, Marsh, but I think with the help of her sons who, by the way, are going to help you tonight, we can manage to put her behind the wheel of a better car. Andrea and I just gave her son, Jason, the Jeep Cherokee that was her dad's, and I'd be more than happy to pay you something for the Civic since you hardly know her."

"Don't be silly, Cory. She seemed like such a gracious lady, and the Police Chief told me about her husband being injured and confined to a wheelchair. I'd be honored to be able to help the family. How old is Jason and the other boy who will be helping me?"

"Jason is 18, or maybe close to 19, and was planning to start college this Fall until another boy walked off with the money he'd worked for and saved all summer. The money was found and has been returned, but he has decided to work the rest of this school year and enroll in college next Fall. He has a scholarship for part of his tuition, but when I saw his car, I was going to buy him one for Christmas until Andrea wanted him to have the Cherokee instead. He received it a little early because his brakes failed, he grazed another car, and then hit a light pole. He is such a great kid, and his brother, Sam, is the other one who will help. He's almost 16. No, that's not right, he just turned 16 recently. I've called and they'll be at your cottage around 7 o'clock. But why were you talking to the Police Chief?"

"I wondered if you'd caught that," Marshall chuckled. "I was raised in a very small town in Kentucky, and I learned that if you want to find anyone to help you do something, the Police Chief is the one to contact. I knew I couldn't ask you or Andrea, or even Donna, as it would've been 'I'll take care of that' so I went to the Chief He's really a great guy and I look forward to getting to know him better."

"Yea, he really is a good Police Chief, but you'll have to hear the story sometime of how he was in cahoots with Andrea's dad and my best man to make sure Andrea would run to me for protection after we'd met. It's funny now, but at the time it was terrifying."

"That sounds like a very interesting story, but I guess I'd better be getting over to the cottage if the boys are going to be there at 7 o'clock. I'm sorry I can't help you clean up the dishes tonight, but I'll be around to help from now on, if I'm invited, except on moving day," he chuckled as he headed for the door.

"Oh, that reminds me, Marshall, I haven't even talked to Cory about this yet, but when I met with the wedding coordinator the other day, she asked if we had an usher. I wondered if you would be willing to do that for us. I'm sure Cory would've preferred you being his best man, but that would be a little hard to change now."

"I understand that, Andrea, and I'd love to be the usher and even walk you down the aisle, if you'd like to have an escort. I couldn't take the place of that father of yours, but I'd be honored to place your hand in Cory's as you begin your wedding vows."

With tears running down her cheeks, Andrea ran into Marshall's arms and then softly whispered, "I'm so glad you've come, Marshall. God is certainly watching out for us."

∽

The girls had gotten the kitchen cleaned up, and then Donna had gone home, but Cory couldn't sit still and finally insisted that they drive over to the cottage and see what was going on. Andrea gave in after he promised that he would not expose himself to the cold night air and would not lift a finger to help.

They could see the boys entering the house with the bed frame as they approached, and they were back out in a few minutes to get the box springs and mattress. They could see that it was a twin size which had made it a little easier to get into the van. The boys had both smiled and waved at them as they pulled into the driveway a little ways back behind the van. Jason had parked the Cherokee in the street.

"Do you suppose he has the heat turned on?" Cory asked and Andrea knew exactly why the question had been asked.

"Let me go see, Cory, because you won't be able to relax until you've seen the inside of that cottage and can see for yourself just how much he actually got in that van of his." She exited the car and scooted to the door behind Jason and Sam who were now carrying a rather large recliner. *How in the world did he get that in the van along with the bed and mattress?*

When she got inside, she could feel the warmth of the logs burning in the fireplace, and it was so cozy as Jason and Sam placed the chair beside a table with a beautiful lamp shining an invitation to all. She just shook her head.

Marshall walked in from the kitchen and had a big smile on his face. "I knew the two of you couldn't stay away so I started the fire. Are you going to let Cory come in?"

"Yes, of course. I'll go get him."

"Let me, Andrea. If you'd like to do something, I need some help deciding where to put the silverware, dishes, and pans in relation to the food items, the stove, and the fridge. Would you like to help me with that?"

"Sure. You go get Cory and I'll take a look around the kitchen." When she got to the kitchen, however, she couldn't believe the things he had in there. *Where in the world did he put all this in that van?* The kitchen was actually similar to her own, so it was no problem to give suggestions to the convenient placing of things when Marshall returned with Cory.

The boys were finished, too, and had big smiles on their faces. "Mr. Calhoun, we want to thank you for asking us to help Mr. Walker tonight. He really knows how to pack a van," Jason laughed. "Is there anything else you need us to help with, Mr. Walker? Otherwise, we'll get out of your way."

"I'm impressed with your help tonight, Guys, and I was wondering if you'd like to help when the moving van comes next Friday? Their schedule appears to have them arriving sometime in the afternoon. He'll have a helper with him, but I thought it might get done faster if there were one or two more."

"We'd love to help. I'll come when I get off work, and Sam can come after school."

"Great, I'll look forward to seeing you then. Oh, just a second. Cory, did you want to say something to the boys now or were you going to take care of that later?"

"I think we should wait on that, Marsh, but I will tell you guys that we'll most likely need your help again soon concerning something we'd like to do for your parents." He then watched with interest how the eyes of both boys sparkled as they couldn't hide their love for their mom and dad.

When Marshall tried to pay them for helping, however, they were refusing to take anything until Cory told them they were entitled to it, and they wouldn't be able to help them again if they were going to be stubborn about this. "There are things you need or want, or a college fund to add to, so don't turn down pay for doing a good job."

"Thanks again, Mr. Calhoun, but there must be some way we can repay you."

"Someday there may be, but right now Mr. Walker is paying you for helping him unload his van so he can sleep here tonight and have a fairly comfortable place to stay until the rest of his furniture gets here. Take it with his thanks and have a good night."

Accepting a number of bills in wide-eyed amazement, they both responded almost in unison, "Thank you, Mr. Walker, and we'll see you next Friday. Goodnight."

"If most of the people in this town are like the ones I've met so far, I know I'm going to be very, very happy here," Marshall remarked with a sigh as he watched the boys get into the Cherokee and slowly drive away.

# Chapter Nineteen

Marshall had offered to fix some coffee, the only thing he had in the house so far, but Cory and Andrea elected to call it a night. Cory was getting tired again and didn't want to chance a recurrence of the flu.

"I'll keep myself busy tomorrow stocking the pantry and refrigerator," Marshall told them as they were preparing to leave, "but I'd like to join you at church on Sunday. I want to get acquainted and involved as soon as possible since my church has been pretty much my life since Jaylene died. I'm sure I wouldn't have made it without my faith and my work since I had considered my life over when I had to face it alone. The pastor's sermons each week seemed to contain just what I needed to hear, so I started having personal meetings with him almost every week. It was really a great help and I'm hoping the pastor here is also easy to talk to."

"We like Pastor Avery very much, but we haven't needed to talk to him one on one. I sure hope you find him sufficient for your needs," Cory replied.

"I didn't mean to get into all that," he chuckled, "but I was actually leading up to one more favor I need. I was wondering if one or both of you would consider helping me, or maybe I could ask Jason. I need someone to go to Boston with me this Sunday, after the service, and drive the Honda down here. I was going to have them put it on the truck, but they had two loads already going on so there wasn't room for the car. Of course, I could've waited an extra week or so for another truck to bring my things, but I thought this was more to my liking."

"I should be all right by Sunday to go with you unless you'd like to let Jason make a little more money," Cory chuckled.

"I wouldn't mind that, but I thought it would give us a chance to talk over a few things before you're married and run away on your honeymoon, but I guess we still have a couple of weeks to do that. When is your mom and Sissy coming? I'm really looking forward to seeing them. It's been such a long time."

"They're coming a week from Sunday after they attend their church services. I haven't had a chance to tell them yet that you're here so it will be a big surprise for them." He could only take a glance at Andrea, who had that smug look on her face, and he had to grin.

"Yea, you'd better keep me a secret, Cory. They might decide to stay home if they know I'm going to be here," he chuckled.

"You were always a big hit with Mom, but I'm not so sure about Sissy," he retorted with a chuckle. "Okay, I'll plan on going with you Sunday afternoon, Marsh, but I'm ready for some more shut-eye right now. Call me, if you need anything. Thanks for showing up just when I needed you and for making this your new home. I need to thank God, too, for making it a part of His plan. Goodnight for now."

"Goodnight, Guys, and thank you for everything you've done for me."

❧

Saturday morning found Cory revived and ready to tackle the world. He decided to go down to the office and check his schedule for next week and also make a list of things he had to be sure to discuss with Marsh. As he was studying a lien that had been filed against an estate, he heard a rapping on the front door. *Now, who could it be this time?* He was smiling, however, when he opened the door and invited Bryan Munson to come in. "What brings you by on a Saturday?" he asked.

"I was hoping you'd be here because my classes don't allow me to come during your office hours, and I wanted to pay you for the time you've spent with me. I did talk to your secretary the other day and told her Marilee and I are working out our differences. Things are really going pretty well. I think the counseling sessions are helping, but it's a struggle to know, sometimes, what she really wants from our marriage. She's been willing to go to church with me, something the counselor suggested, and it seems to make her more willing to sit down and open up to me about what is troubling her."

"I'm usually not here on Saturday, but I had the flu for a couple of days so I came in to see what I had on my desk for next week, I'm so glad I was here today when you came by because I've wanted to discuss something with you. I don't know if it would help or not, but Andrea and I are getting married on the Saturday after Thanksgiving, and I just thought that maybe attending a wedding, where love is very visible, might help Marilee see how love and marriage can be wonderful together. Of course, I could be wrong—it might make her regret eloping and missing out on having a church wedding."

"Congratulations, Mr. Calhoun, you're getting a wonderful girl, but Marilee always said she didn't want the hassle of a church wedding, and she actually was the one who suggested we elope. Are you sure it will be all right if we come to your wedding? I think she'd really enjoy it because she finally told me that one reason she didn't want a church wedding was because her family does not believe in going to church, she had never been to a church wedding, and so she wasn't familiar with the procedure. If she were to decide, after we've been to your wedding, that she wants to renew our vows in a church setting, I'd be more than happy to see that she gets that chance."

"Well, we'd love to have you come, and we'd also love to help you if you decide to have a church ceremony. Ours is at 3 o'clock in the chapel of the First Protestant Church, and the reception will be in the banquet room of Cathy's Bistro."

"That chapel doesn't hold too many people. Are you sure we won't be intruding?"

Not succeeding in holding back a chuckle, Cory explained, "We originally thought we would only have about six people in the pews, but we are getting it filled up by going out, like in the Bible, and inviting all to come in. That's not quite what happened, but you get what I mean. Andrea was beginning to think I was going to invite the whole town. However, she knows I was planning to invite you and Marilee, and she does approve. Andrea and I are both rather new in town, by ordinary standards, plus we have very few relatives that we can invite. Both of her parents are gone and she was an only child. My dad has also been gone since I was little, so we'd be honored to have you come."

"We'll be there, but now back to my purpose for coming. What do I owe you for the time you've spent with me? It should be even more since you've given me this time today."

"You owe me nothing, Bryan, because I didn't really do anything. I didn't even get a meeting with Andrea set up before you were back with a solution of your own. I'm just so pleased that you're back together and working on a lasting relationship. Andrea and I will keep you in our prayers and look forward to seeing you on the 25th."

"Thanks, Mr. Calhoun, you don't realize how much your encouragement has meant to me. I'm so glad I decided to come see you. You have a nice Thanksgiving and we'll be at your wedding to help you celebrate."

"Bryan, do you have plans to be with family on Thanksgiving?"

Hesitating, Bryan's face told Cory what he was going to say. "No, Mr. Calhoun, both of our families have pretty much ignored us since we eloped, but we'll be together and that will be enough to be thankful for."

"No, Bryan, that absolutely and definitely won't be enough. Do you know where Andrea's cottage is located?"

When Bryan nodded, Cory continued, "You two be there about noon on Turkey Day. I'm not sure what time we're eating, but there will be people there who are thankful for the love of family and will welcome you with open arms. I mean it, Bryan, we want you there, so don't disappoint us."

With tears in his eyes, Bryan could only whisper a 'Thank You' as he opened the door and disappeared down the street.

*Forgive me, Andrea, for adding two more to your already heavy burden, but I just couldn't let that young couple feel unloved on Thanksgiving Day.*

Sitting back down at his desk, Cory was reflecting on all the extraordinary events that had happened since Andrea had come into his life, when the phone started ringing. He felt quite sure she was checking on him, so he let it ring four times before answering as if he were out of breath.

"Cory, are you all right? You sound winded," he heard his mother ask.

"Hey, Mom, how'd you know to call me here? You know I'm usually not in the office on Saturdays."

"Elimination, My Dear. I called your apartment, and then I called Andrea. She told me you might be at the office since you'd been sick part of Thursday and yesterday. I'm so sorry to hear that, Dear. You are hardly ever sick."

"Well, I guess I'm just getting old, feeble, and forgetful. I forgot to get my flu shot this year. If I don't get a wife to take care of me soon, I may have to recruit you to be my nurse," he laughed. "So, what can I do for you today?"

"Nothing, really—I just wanted to hear that sweet unattached voice one or two more times before it finally becomes a husband and a daddy, I hope. You know how much I want to become a grandmother."

"Oh, yes, how well I remember that you want to be a grandmother. Well, take heart, Mrs. Calhoun, because I think the future Mrs. Calhoun has some intentions along that same line. She is already planning quite an addition to the cottage to accommodate her desire to have more than one little bundle to require those diaper changes, nighttime feedings, the towel over the shoulder for burping sessions, not to mention walking the floor with a fussy little cherub."

"Cory Calhoun, shame on you. I love that girl before I've even met her! I wish time would pass a little more quickly."

"Well, you could come sooner, and we'd get to visit a little longer before Andrea and I leave on our honeymoon and start working on those grandbabies you want."

"We would, Dear, but Sissy has a book signing in Philly next Wednesday through the lunch hour on Friday, so Sunday it has to be."

"We're looking forward to it. Is Sissy still planning to stay at Andrea's?"

"She's ecstatic about the whole thing. Of course, we're both looking forward to seeing with our own eyes that you are finally married."

"Yea, one big worry off your mind, even though I'm not really that old, but how about getting Sissy married? Actually, I may have a great big surprise for the two of you when you get here. Is it definitely all right with the library that you take the month off?"

"Oh, yes, that's all set, but what is this surprise? You can't leave me dangling like that, Cory."

He couldn't help chuckling. "Oh, I really could, Mom, but I won't if you'll promise not to mention it to Sissy."

"My lips are sealed and she isn't here right now to overhear, so please, Cory, hurry and tell me what it is."

>

"Marshall Walker has bought a cottage just down the street from Andrea's and is moving here since resigning his position at the law firm. He says he got burned out from trying to bury his sorrow in work, but he does want to help me in the office, just for a little something to do besides some fishing, getting a tan, and finding a pretty lady to be his wife. He has asked about you and Sissy, and he's looking forward to seeing you both again. You do remember that he lost his wife to cancer 16 months ago?"

"Yes, I remember, Cory, and he was such a nice young man. Do you think he might really be interested in Sissy seriously?"

"He just said he was going to check things out at Thanksgiving. He'll be spending the day with us."

"How exciting! You've certainly made my day, Dear. It's really going to be a long week now with this news that I can't talk about, but we'll see you soon. Is Andrea sure about having all of us for Thanksgiving?"

"Yes, she'll be fine. I think she'll put Sissy to work a little helping."

"Sissy will love that. Bye for now, and please give Andrea our love."

"Will do. Bye, Mom. I love you."

>>                                                          >>

## Chapter Twenty

Cory was still chuckling at his mother's reaction to his news while he was dialing Andrea's number. "Hey, Sweetheart, how's your day going?" he asked when she had been a little slow to answer.

"Oh, Cory, I'm having so much fun. I got a big piece of paper and I've been drawing my ideas for the renovation to the cottage. I think the present floor plan is great and is in very good shape. Dad remodeled the master bedroom, you know, and also did extensive work in the kitchen. I've seen several features in magazines that I've liked so my thought is to add a two-car attached garage to the south of the current house but which would extend out past the front of the cottage. Behind it, along the living room, dining room and kitchen, there'd be a storage space as part of the garage, a big family room, and a large screened-in porch.

The addition upstairs would create four bedrooms, a playroom and two storage areas, plus there would be a look-over (or whatever you call it) from the play area down to the family room. The present door in the kitchen would open to the porch. I've thought about adding a counter and stools along the island stove for informal snacks and breakfasts instead of the small table and chairs we have now. My present bedroom could become a den, a home office or a nursery. Cory, can you follow my ramblings?" she giggled. "I'm also imagining the old garage becoming a bathhouse, and we'd install a pool with a shallow end, of course, for our little ones. Cory, are you even listening?"

"Yes, Sweetie, I'm listening and I'm intrigued. You do realize, don't you, that you'll have to consider what this addition will do to the present appearance of the house, if you want to keep the cottage look? You don't want to add anything too modern to go with the original cottage. That, of course, is Mr. Anderson's expertise. I'm just rather surprised you have time for all that with so many other things you have to do in such a short time before Thanksgiving and the wedding."

"Oh, I'm going to put this away now and make a list of things I have to do with Susan and Grace next week before your mom and sister get here. The following week will be busy getting Thanksgiving dinner preparations made. However, if you get a chance to look at the plans I've drawn, and like them, I may talk to Mr. Anderson before we leave on our trip. That way, he may be able to get to ours before he starts on the townhouses. But, Cory, have you decided where you're taking me yet, or are you going to continue to keep me in the dark?"

"Just plan for nice warm days and a secret place on one of the beautiful Caribbean Islands, and the future Mrs. Calhoun will be set to enjoy her honeymoon."

"I guess that's enough information to help me pack all my alluring outfits in my great big suitcase," she mused.

"My plans don't include you wearing too many clothes, Andrea, My Dear," he very smugly laughed. "Maybe you could just plan to carry a tote bag."

"Cory, you stop talking that way or I may decide you're too naughty for me to even associate with," she giggled. "By the way, did your mother reach you?"

"Yes, Sweetie, and her thoughts are dwelling on you and me getting pretty cozy, too, so she can become a grandmother."

"Oh no, Cory, not immediately! We need time to do things together, like a big long cruise on the boat, or maybe even two or three, before we start a family when we'll have to share our time with little ones. We really want to know each other well before we do that, don't you think? We'll also want to have the cottage addition completed before we bring any babies into the world."

"That's another one of your most brilliant ideas, Sweetheart. With you so engrossed with enlarging the cottage, I was beginning to wonder if you really did plan to start our family right away. I'm so glad to learn that you want my company for something other than giving you morning sickness," he chuckled. "But to change the subject once again, Andrea, how many can you seat comfortably at the table?" he asked almost in a whisper.

"Cory Calhoun, what have you done now?" she moaned. "I can seat twelve, but we already have eight coming, so how many more have you invited?" She exhaled a sigh that he could hear loud and clear.

He very quietly proceeded to tell her about Bryan's visit and that he'd learned that he and Marilee wouldn't have a family to join on Thanksgiving Day. She readily agreed that he'd done the right thing. "For that situation I would've set up another table because it is just so sad to think parents would ignore their children, especially on holidays."

"Thanks, Sweetie, I felt you'd approve so I told Bryan that you knew I was going to invite them. Now I think I'll chase Marshall down, since he doesn't have his phone installed yet and I forgot to ask for his cell number. I want to find out exactly what his plans are for tomorrow. I was thinking we could go to the early service and then head out so we wouldn't be quite so late getting back. Were you wanting to ride along?"

"Would you mind if I stayed here, Cory? I'd like to go to the later service, and then I can have a meal ready when you two get back. I have some things I need to get done before your mom and Sissy come, and definitely plan the next two weeks."

"I'll drop by after I talk to Marsh, and maybe I can look at the drawing then. I love you, Sweetheart."

"I love you, too. See you later."

*A warm secret spot in the Caribbean, he says. Most of the places are warm, so it must be the 'secret spot' I need to concentrate on. Did he find a quiet secluded hideaway, or is 'secret' in its name. Whatever, it's not going to be easy to find light-weight clothes around here in November, so I'll go through my summer clothes and check those latest purchases. I found some real cute things on sale, just before I met Cory, and I didn't even wear some of them. I think I have all I'll need, and I can start filling my suitcase today.*

She was truly into the selecting process when she heard, "Honey, where are you? Marsh and I thought we'd get something to eat. Will you join us?"

Hurrying out of her bedroom and quickly closing the door, she glanced at her watch as she smiled a little sheepishly. "I didn't realize it had gotten so late. I'm sorry I don't have anything fixed, so where were you planning to go?"

"Probably just to the Cafe or the Chinese Restaurant," Cory answered as he was studying her face. "What have you been doing, Andrea, that you had to shut the bedroom door when we arrived? You're looking a little guilty about something so I think I'll check on what, or who, is on the other side of that door." He started toward the closed door, but Andrea quickly stationed herself in front of it.

"No, you aren't going in there, Cory. If you must know, I was just getting some of my summer clothes out for the trip, even though it's none of your business. I am taking a bunch of clothes, no matter what you say."

"Oh," Cory remarked as he backed away. He felt so embarrassed he wanted to run out the door, but he made it worse by asking, "You don't have a guy hiding in there, do you?"

With that remark, Marshall couldn't hold back his laughter. "The green-eyed monster has arrived, Andrea, so you'd better be ready for interrogations whenever you're trying to keep a secret, unless you have a very convincing straight face that you can use. So far, I haven't seen your capability to display anything other than honesty, and from all my past experiences, I know most attorneys are always looking for clues, so it isn't easy to surprise them. But, Cory, are you really going to insist on seeing her room? You need to learn to have just a little more trust. Come on, let's go eat."

As Marshall was still chuckling, Cory gave a somewhat amused Andrea a little apologetic smile as he took her in his arms, gave her a quick kiss, and whispered, "I'm so sorry, Sweetheart." Then, with her hand in his, they headed toward Marshall's van for the trip to a restaurant and some food for their empty stomachs.

Andrea was having a cup of coffee and looking at the paper Sunday morning when she heard a short toot and glanced up just in time to see Marshall's van going by. *They're on their way, Dear Jesus, and I ask that you please keep them safe in your arms while they are on the highways today.*

She did the usual morning chores and then enjoyed the 11 a.m. service. As she was leaving the church, she saw the Andersons and went over to greet them. She was even a little surprised at herself when she started telling them about the addition she wanted to put on the cottage and asking Mr. Anderson if he would have time to draw some plans for her. "I've made an attempt to put my ideas in a drawing. Cory saw them last night but only gave me his approval to talk to you because he's afraid it will take away the cottage look. If you have to make some changes to keep the cottage look, that's OK, but we'll need the additional space."

"I'll be happy to see what I can do for you, Andrea. With all my new equipment, I'm really getting anxious to see what I really *can* do. Would you like to bring your drawing over this afternoon?"

"I hate to bother you on a Sunday, but with Thanksgiving and the wedding coming up so soon, if I could bring it to you today, it would certainly help me out and you could take your time with it. If other work needs to be done, just put mine aside because Cory and I will be on our honeymoon for awhile and probably won't want to get started on the addition until Spring at the earliest. I understand that Mr. Capland is talking to you about the plans for the sub-division that we're working on, and that should be the first priority."

"Yes, he has seen me, Andrea, and I need to thank you for making that a part of the conditions before you would invest. You and Mr. Calhoun have gone way beyond anything we could've imagined to make our life better, and we're certainly indebted to you. Letting me draw your plans will be a pleasure."

"Oh, you're not doing this for free, Mr. Anderson. If that's what you're thinking, I won't let you do it. Cory and I have the means now, and we get great pleasure by helping others."

"Well, all these wonderful things happening in our lives and our town wouldn't have been possible without our Lord bringing your father here first, and now you and that great Cory Calhoun, so we'll just let Him continue to bless us, if it be His will."

"That's better," she smiled at the family, "and I'll bring my feeble attempt at drawing over to you this afternoon. Cory and his friend, Marshall, are on their way to Boston to get a few of his things, so I have a few free hours today except to have a meal ready for them when they get back."

The time spent that afternoon was very enlightening as Mr. Anderson took time to explain what her drawings would do to the present cottage if the addition were to be built according to her design.

"First," he'd said, "Cory is right. The garage being in the front of the house would completely ruin the cottage look since that style of construction has only been used in the last 25 to maybe 50 years on modern homes while your cottage is more like 80 to 90 years old. Another factor that you probably didn't consider is that the continuation of the garage and storage area closes off your two living room windows which I'm sure you would hate when you started living in there. Your driveway could come up that side of the house and a storage area could be added inside the garage at the back, however.

Then there's your idea of the two-story family room with the railing across the play area upstairs. This is not only too modern for your cottage, Andrea, but also too dangerous for small children. Most of those railings are along a hallway or a walkway, but not where children would be running and playing without a thought of the danger. I'm also thinking about how much more use you'd get out of a sunroom instead of just a screened in porch, although your family room might suffice. However, it could possibly serve as the play room while a sunroom with windows and screens could be a retreat for adults.

Now, would you let me draw up some plans trying to keep it a cottage? If it doesn't meet your approval, we can try again or you may want to accept the fact that your cottage will have to become a larger family home if you want as much extra space as you've shown in your drawing. And let me ask you about another idea that just came to me. Would you consider extending your present front porch around the corner of the house and then let it go on across the front of the family room? I think it might be a very attractive way to connect the two sections of the house, so to speak, and keep the desired vintage."

"All of your ideas sound so exciting, Mr. Anderson. Thanks so much for taking the time to explain all this to me. I'll talk to Cory and then try to get back to you, but I'll look forward to seeing your plans and drawings. I'd better let you have some time with your family now, though, and I need to get home so I'll have time to get a meal prepared. Thanks again."

Andrea had returned from the Anderson's about 3 o'clock, and while she was preparing the pork roast for the oven and chopping the ingredients for a Waldorf salad, she'd been listening to music on the radio and singing along. All of a sudden, they broke in with a News Alert and announced that there had been an accident on I-93, just north of Braintree. She listened more closely as they reported one death and two others were now being airlifted to a Boston hospital.

She rushed to the phone and dialed Cory's cell phone, but there was no answer. She tried to keep calm while trying to rationalize why he wouldn't answer his phone. *Did he forget to take it with him, is he away from the car helping at the scene, or Dear God, could he have been involved? Is he one of the injured being airlifted or is he the fatality?*

"What can I do?" she moaned as she forced herself to remain focused on putting the roast in the oven and the salad in the refrigerator. She tried the cell phone number again but still no answer. She finally curled up on the couch as she realized she was really shaking with fright. *Andrea, get yourself under control,* she urged as she listened for more news on the injured. She heard that a pickup truck was one of the vehicles involved, but nothing on the other one. She couldn't control the tears that were running down her cheeks. She tried calling him once more with no success.

She kept listening for up-to-date information, but there was no more news on the condition of the victims. She was so distraught by now that she didn't hear the door open or see Cory and Marshall come in.

Cory couldn't believe his eyes as he walked into the living room and found her on the couch shaking and crying uncontrollably. He fell on his knees in front of her. "Honey, what is wrong?" he asked, but before she could answer, he heard the radio stating that another of the injured had died on the way to the hospital. He and Marshall had heard the ambulances and squad car sirens, and had seen the flashing lights behind them, but they had been past the accident scene and in no danger whatsoever.

For an instant, Andrea looked at him as if she was looking right through him, and then she screamed, "Oh, Cory, you're alive," and she threw her arms around his neck so tightly he had to pry them loose so he could breathe.

"Honey, why were you so affected by this accident report? Why didn't you just call me if you were concerned?"

She drew away from him and just stared, and then all of a sudden, she slapped his face hard and screamed at him again. "I did, Cory Calhoun, and you didn't answer. I called you two or three times and then I was sure you were hurt or dead. Why didn't you answer your phone, or didn't you even take it with you?"

"It didn't ring, Andrea," he replied rather obstinately. "You must've been so upset you dialed the wrong number because it is right here in my pocket." He slowly pulled it out to show her, but when he looked at it, he gulped. "Oops, I'm so sorry, Sweetheart, it needs to be charged. I guess I forgot to plug it in last night." He tried to take her in his arms, but she just shoved him away causing him to sit down clumsily on the floor.

She stomped into the kitchen while wiping her eyes and blowing her nose. Starting to set the table, she was mumbling that everything would've been ready if a certain person had been the least bit competent.

Marshall, of course, had stood watching the whole exchange and couldn't hold back a few chuckles as Cory sat there on the floor. Tears were glistening in Cory's eyes while he was shaking his head.

"Am I really ready for marriage, Marsh? It seems I always succeed in creating a big problem or, at least, a worry for her."

"You're going to be fine, Cory. Marriage is based on gives and takes although it looks like the two of you may have more than your share. You won't have to worry about a humdrum type of togetherness, however. I must say that I can't blame her for the reaction you got this time, though. You *were* somewhat negligent."

"Yeah, I know," he mumbled as he raised himself off the floor and into a standing position with one of those limber athletic maneuvers. "Why don't you check out the TV, if you want, while I see if I can either help in the kitchen or be thrown out again." He was somehow able to grin before he headed for the war zone with his white handkerchief waving in his hand.

# Chapter Twenty-One

When Andrea had called Grace to postpone their shopping trip last Friday when Cory was sick, they'd decided they would again try the little bridal shop in town on Monday, if possible, just on the chance they could find something and not have to drive to Plymouth or even Boston. If they couldn't find what they liked, they'd still have time to go to the other two.

So, when they entered the small shop called Bride's Etc., they really weren't expecting to find the large selection they found, which pleasantly surprised them. The manager, who looked as if she could've been a model a few years back, welcomed them. When she noticed their true interest, she explained that this shop was actually owned by a large bridal shop in Boston, and even though they don't carry all sizes in each style, they could have it overnight from the main store.

After asking a few questions about the wedding and what style of dress Andrea was interested in, she said, "Let's look at what we have in your size first," as she walked toward one of the displays. "Do you usually wear a Size 2 or Size 4?"

"It usually depends on the style and the brand," Andrea smiled, "but let's start with the 4's." She and Grace liked three of the seven gowns, but they soon discovered they'd have to look at the 2's. They found four to try in that group, but when Andrea modeled the second one, Grace and the clerk were oohing and aahing. It was a darling floor-length taffeta sheath that was sleeveless, but it was covered with a delicate silky lace which formed a nice standup collar, snug long sleeves, and also extended over the short chapel train. It fit beautifully without a single alteration required. Andrea also loved the dress and how it fit her, so she was thrilled that her search was over. She had her wedding gown.

When they started looking for Grace's dress, a beautiful silk dress in light pumpkin which was styled with a boat neckline, an empire waist, elbow length sleeves, and a slightly flared ankle-length skirt caught their attention. It was perfect for the season and they thought it would be striking on Grace with her dark hair and eyes. While she was trying on the dress, Andrea happened to notice the lingerie section and wandered over to take a look. Grace soon joined her, as she was modeling the dress, and heard Andrea giggling.

"What's so funny?" she asked.

"Oh, I was just thinking about Cory's remark to me that his honeymoon plans didn't include me wearing too many clothes."

"That may be true, Andrea, but I found a lot of the fun was making Roger take them off of me. You'll need some very enticing gowns and teddies. Now, this one would certainly raise some eyebrows," she grinned as she held up a full-length see-thru gown and negligee.

"And I thought I'd just take my old worn-thin night gowns that he keeps catching me in. He seems to enjoy trying to see through those," she laughed.

They were thrilled that they had decided to shop right here in town, and they soon had selected a nice supply of teddies, a short slip-style gown with a matching robe, and a simply gorgeous long gown with negligee, all of which they took with them so Andrea could get them in her suitcase without Cory seeing them. They would pick up the wedding dresses on the Friday before the wedding since Grace's needed just a few little alterations. They were promised that both would be ready for them to walk down the aisle although Grace would be called in for a fitting when it had been altered.

They then stopped at the flower shop because Andrea wanted her bouquet to match the color of Grace's dress, if possible, and the clerk had given them a swatch of the material which made it so much easier for the florist. They also made the final decision on the color of flowers Grace would carry, the corsages and the boutonnieres.

They decided to have lunch at Cathy's Bistro and see if they could look at the banquet room where the reception was going to be. Satisfied, they called it a day although Andrea had asked Grace if she and Roger would come for dinner. It proved to be a wonderful evening and they all felt that a lasting friendship was being formed and spending time with each other would be great.

❧

The rest of the week passed quickly. Andrea had met with Susan twice to make sure all the wedding plans were complete, and by Sunday afternoon she felt she was ready for Cory's mother and sister to arrive. Although she'd been a little nervous as she anticipated meeting them, it was a thrill when they finally arrived, and they had a great time as Roger, Grace, Marshall and Donna joined them for some light snacks before going to dinner. Mrs. Calhoun had kept her promise to Cory, so Sissy was really surprised when Marshall walked in the door. She was very shy, or maybe a little distant toward him, but Marshall proved to be a great conversationalist, and Andrea felt it wasn't long until he had Sissy eating out of his hand, so to speak.

Sissy was a wonderful help as they handled the meals each day and also made the final plans for the Thanksgiving dinner. Sissy practiced with the organist on Tuesday and Cory fixed chicken on the grill while Andrea fixed parsley-buttered potatoes and tossed a nice lettuce salad. Wednesday night they had pizza brought in.

There was a Thanksgiving Day service at the church Thursday morning and everyone had decided they would like to go except Cory. He was a little concerned about Bryan and Marilee coming and finding no one at home, so he elected to pass the service. Marshall was there and slipped in beside Sissy which had her mother and Andrea smiling big time. Roger and Grace had also joined them, as they had been doing since returning from Boston. It was a very moving service as lay persons told of their past, how they had become Christians and were so thankful that God was now in charge of their lives.

Bryan and Marilee were at the cottage, when they returned, but they learned that they had been in the back pew of the church for most of the service. Bryan hadn't seen Andrea since he didn't recognize the ones she was with. Grinning, he remarked, "We had slipped out early because we didn't want to be late arriving for the wonderful smells coming from the kitchen." The big turkey was certainly giving off a delicious aroma.

What a wonderful day it turned out to be. Everyone was so warm and gracious, and Marshall had somehow convinced Sissy to go with him to see his cottage because he felt he needed some help arranging his furniture. There was a big grin on his face as he glanced at Cory, but he didn't happen to see the smiles on the faces of Mrs. Calhoun, Donna, and of course, Andrea. Roger and Grace departed early so she could really get rested up before the big weekend. Later, after enjoying some more pie and coffee, Bryan, Marilee, and Donna also scooted along. Mrs.Calhoun was soon asleep with a book across her lap, while Andrea and Cory finished cleaning up the kitchen.

The rehearsal had gone well Friday night and now the big day was here. Andrea was so nervous, but Sissy was very good at fixing hair and got to telling stories about her writing and travels. She had Andrea laughing, relaxing and elated as she watched herself being transformed in the mirror. Sissy had swirled most of her hair into a pretty bun on top of her head with tendrils touching the sides of her face and down the back of her neck.

Susan was to pick up the dresses and have them and all the flowers waiting as each person arrived at the church. Andrea and Sissy arrived early enough to get a glimpse of the chapel and were simply amazed at its beauty. The candles in the candelabra were glowing, accented with entwined ivory roses, baby's breath and lush greenery. Each pew had a large bow of ivory and pumpkin ribbons, and the Unity Candle was surrounded with tiny ivory rose buds. The individual bride and groom candles were waiting to be lit my Mrs. Calhoun, who will be escorted to the altar by Marshall, and then seated in her pew. He will join her after placing Andrea's hand in Cory's.

Sissy and Susan helped Andrea and Grace slip into their dresses. At 2:45 the organist began to play several traditional wedding songs, and Sissy took her place near the organ just before Mrs.Calhoun came forward to light the bride and groom candles. At 2:55 Cory and Roger came in with Pastor Avery. Sissy then stood and sang "The First Time I Saw You Was The Moment I Loved You," a song that was in a book she'd read and which she felt told exactly what had happened to her brother. It was her special gift to him.

As he listened to the words, Cory couldn't imagine a song had been written that told his reaction to meeting Andrea so well. He thought perhaps Sissy had written it herself, but his attention turned quickly to the aisle as Grace was entering, looking quite stunning in her light pumpkin dress and carrying a cascade of ivory roses.

And then he saw Andrea, escorted by his very handsome friend, Marshall Walker, but he only had eyes for his bride-to-be. She looked absolutely adorable in her taffeta and lace gown and a short veil held in place by a small circlet of pearls. Her bridal bouquet consisted of one large white lily encircled with roses in the exact color of Grace's dress and cascading to a single bud. She was wearing his gift of a single strand of pearls and a pair of dangling earrings which added the perfect touch to her wedding outfit.

Marshall expertly kept her moving toward the front of the church as he felt a slight hesitation in her step and wondered if she might be thinking about dashing back out the door. "You'll be fine," he whispered as he squeezed her arm and gave her the smile she had come to know and appreciate in the short time since he'd arrived in Sparlin.

She suddenly found herself at the altar and Marshall was placing her shaking hand in Cory's outstretched one. One look at her soon-to-be husband made her smile and realize this was exactly where she wanted to be, but she'd had to stifle a little giggle when she saw him smiling and his long, gorgeous eyelashes were fluttering at her.

The opening remarks were made by Pastor Avery and then Sissy sang "God By My Side" which brought tears to Andrea's eyes. It seemed to confirm Cory's faith that it was God's plan for them to be together, even when she was so insecure, and, of course, she couldn't forget that her father had had a hand in it, too.

The day I saw you standing there,

I knew God was by my side,
And if my faith could be strong enough,
You would someday be my bride.

With sunlight shining in your eyes,
Or the moonlight on your face,
For me to find someone as sweet as you,
I had relied upon His grace.

Not by chance or a human scheme,
Only God's hand holding fast
To His plan for you and me, My Love,
As we shared what was our past.

And now I'm thanking Him, My Dear,
As I have you at my side.
We can face the future together
With God as our perfect guide.

Andrea could hardly believe that she had answered "I Do" when she was supposed to and also repeated her vows before she heard the pastor's instructions to kneel. Sissy's singing of 'The Lord's Prayer' was the part of the service that she would never forget, however, because it was the most moving rendition she had ever heard, and she prayed that everyone had been touched as she had. It was also very meaningful when she and Cory lit the Unity Candle together, she heard that they were now husband and wife, and he was kissing her, oh so tenderly.

They danced, they talked with everyone, they cut their cake and had something to eat, and then Cory whispered softly in her ear that they had a plane to catch. "Oh, Cory, I don't know if I'm ready to leave. Is . . ." but his fingers to her lips prevented her from asking all the questions he knew were racing through that head of hers.

"Yes, Sweetie," he continued to whisper, "everything is taken care of, and we are going to the cottage now to change our clothes. Very, very soon we'll be in a secret place, no TV, the lights turned down low, and there will be just you and me making wonderful music, or more likely love, together."

"Well, what are we waiting for?" she giggled as they waved goodbye to everyone and then said hello to each other with a long, passionate kiss when they were outside the door. He held her arm on the way to his car and then they entered into another world—a world that a wonderful man had somehow known was right for both of them.

"Thanks, Dad," they both murmured and then smiled at each other as they drove away to start the rest of their lives together.

>>                                                                   >>

## About the Author

Sally had never traveled extensively, but the one trip she'll always remember is the one she and her husband, J.T., took from Chillicothe, IL down to Biloxi, MS on their 28-1/2 foot Cabin Cruiser. They were on eight rivers and went through twenty locks during their 14 days of sunshine. It was exciting as they cruised on the Illinois, Mississippi, Ohio, and Cumberland rivers before reaching Kentucky Lake. On south from there, they were on the Tennessee River, The Tombigbee Waterway, the Black Warrior and Mobile Rivers which took them into Mobile Bay. They then had a rather scary trip across the Gulf with three to five foot waves giving their small boat and J.T., its captain, all they wanted to handle. It goes without saying that they were very relieved when they saw the entrance to the Broadwater Beach Marina at Biloxi.

They'd seen a 40' Bluewater Yacht at the marina on Mobile Bay, which had been very impressive, and it is the one she remembers as she writes this story.

She grew up in Galesburg, Illinois and lived there for 67 years, except for their trips to the East coast to visit family. She moved to Charlotte, NC and then to Lawrence, KS, but after the death of her husband, she moved back toGalesburg to be near her two sons and their families.